"You'll always belong to me, Elizabeth."

Caleb's voice was a ragged whisper. His hand molded her breast possessively, as if stamping her with his mark. "If you leave me, I'll find you." He spread open her jacket and flicked her shirt buttons out of their buttonholes with startling speed. "I'll find you, and by God, I'll make you need me as much as I need you."

She couldn't catch her breath, couldn't form a coherent thought. Automatically, she pushed on his chest and started to utter some feeble protest. He thwarted her by capturing her lips with his own as his hand slid up to unfasten her bra.

As he gazed at her, the dim light of the shed threw his features into sharp relief, making him look hard and hungry. But his touch was infinitely delicate, a feather stroke as he traced the shape of her breasts, and she found herself reaching for him, needing him. "Caleb—" Her voice broke as he shifted his body to press his arousal more firmly against her.

He raised his head. "Stop me now, Elizabeth." His voice had become a near growl.

She knew what he was saying. *Stop me now, or it will be too late.* She clung to him. "It doesn't matter. Nothing matters except that…it's you."

Dear Reader,

There's something about bad boys that most women respond to on a gut level. It isn't fear alone that raises our pulse and leaves us a trifle breathless. With Temptation's REBELS & ROGUES stories, we get to experience the dark, dangerous, mysterious men from the safety of our favorite reading chair.

I'm proud that *A Hard-Hearted Hero* is part of the REBELS & ROGUES series, and proud also that this book won first place in its category in the Heart of the West national writing contest. I thought it would be a fun challenge to write a modern abduction romance, featuring a maverick commando who'd honed his skills in the army's elite Delta Force. I hope you're ready for a four-alarm read! I'm never shy about exploring the passionate side of my characters' relationships.

I live on Long Island with my husband and two children, and am founder and president of Long Island Romance Writers. I love to hear from my readers—let me know what you think of *A Hard-Hearted Hero*. Write to P.O. Box 1321, North Baldwin, NY 11510-0721 (please include an SASE for a reply).

Happy reading!

Pamela Burford

Books by Pamela Burford

HARLEQUIN TEMPTATION
658—JACKS ARE WILD

HARLEQUIN INTRIGUE
360—HIS SECRET SIDE
420—TWICE BURNED

A HARD-HEARTED HERO
Pamela Burford

Harlequin Books

TORONTO • NEW YORK • LONDON
AMSTERDAM • PARIS • SYDNEY • HAMBURG
STOCKHOLM • ATHENS • TOKYO • MILAN
MADRID • WARSAW • BUDAPEST • AUCKLAND

To my son and technical adviser, Daniel, for patiently sharing his vast expertise on the subject of model rockets

ISBN 0-373-25744-9

A HARD-HEARTED HERO

Copyright © 1997 by Pamela Burford.

This edition published by arrangement with Harlequin Books S.A.

Printed in U.S.A.

1

ELIZABETH NEVER HAD TIME to scream. One moment she was mopping the last toilet stall, looking forward to collapsing on her cot. The next instant strong hands seized her and slammed her back against a wide chest—a wall of hot, breathing steel. A huge gloved hand smothered half her face before she could catch her breath, much less get to her weapon.

She jabbed the mop handle at her unseen assailant, only to have it wrenched from her rubber-gloved hands and plopped into the commode she'd just scrubbed.

She'd known the risks from the moment she joined the Avalon Collective, but she never thought it would happen this soon. Or quite this way.

Now she was going to end up like David.

A strip of duct tape replaced the hand over her mouth. Elizabeth struggled wildly, but the arms pinning her were pure sinew beneath the black sweater sleeves, unyielding as iron bands.

He jerked her arms behind her and tore off her rubber gloves. She felt the shock of cold steel on her wrists, heard the distinctive ratchety sound of handcuffs tightening.

She twisted violently, kicking him with her bare

feet, hoping to throw him off balance, make him lose his footing on the wet floor. No good. He was as immovable as granite.

The tiled room spun crazily as he hoisted her over his massive shoulder. Her forehead collided with the small of his back—and a hard lump she had no trouble identifying as a concealed, holstered firearm.

He placed a hand on the back of her thigh to steady her...and froze. She groaned under her gag, knowing her last hope had just evaporated. She felt him yank off a leather glove. Warm, callused fingers swept under her long, Indian-print skirt and over her bare legs...and between them, despite her efforts to squeeze them together. She felt a chuckle rumble deep in his massive torso as those fingers closed over *her* holster, strapped to her inner thigh.

"Well, I'll be damned...." It was a baritone whisper, half amazed, half amused.

He flipped her skirt up. All the way up. She felt cool air on her bottom, hatefully displayed in her little pink bikini panties. He drew her slim semiautomatic out of the thigh holster. In the process his knuckles fleetingly brushed between her legs, creating a charge of electric heat that made her breath snag. She sensed him checking the safety and examining the gun briefly before pocketing it.

The doorknob to the outer hallway jiggled and Elizabeth whipped her head up, her screams muffled by the duct tape, her long brown hair falling around her face, obscuring her view.

Knocks and irate voices sounded at the closed door. "Who locked this door? Beth, are you still in there?"

He'd locked the door! How had it been possible for a man this size to skulk around a mirrored, tiled room invisibly...soundlessly...while she'd swabbed out the toilets?

Who *was* this guy? She couldn't recall anyone this big and muscular at Avalon—he had to be at least six four—but then perhaps Lugh hired outsiders for nasty little jobs like this.

Shouts came from the other side of the door, more frantic now. "Someone get the key! Where's the key?"

The big guy didn't seem overly concerned. He must have jammed the lock somehow. She heard the grating sound of more duct tape peeling off a roll. He wound it about her ankles—several layers, good and tight. More around her legs, just above her knees, stealing any last remnants of mobility.

Only then did her skirt come back down. After a proprietary pat to her rump.

Ironically, that mild little pat only magnified her horror. She choked back a sob as she realized for the first time that this man might have more in store for her than simple murder.

Now he was on the move, replacing his glove and heading for the window, which must have been how he got in. Past the heavy-duty locks and a state-of-the-art electronic security system. But then she recalled that this was almost certainly an inside job. He eased through the window and leaped several feet to the ground, never once losing his balance, despite his burden.

The damp chill of the October night swallowed them up as he sprinted across **the** grounds of the Avalon Collective, a sixties-style commune in upstate New York, heading for the tree line. He was as swift and graceful as a big cat, but Elizabeth still jounced painfully, her breath coming in harsh little grunts.

He charged into the cover of the woods, dodging and ducking unseen obstacles like some feral beast of the night. Thin tree branches snagged her skirt and scratched her lower legs. Draped over him as she was, Elizabeth could clearly feel his deep, controlled breaths, his steady, powerful heartbeat. The guy wasn't even winded!

At last they squeezed through a fresh gash in the tall chain-link fence—*his* handiwork, no doubt—and emerged onto a gravel road. The world tilted once more as he righted her and propped her against a vehicle—some big, four-wheel-drive thing. She was shaking so hard she could barely stay upright. Her toes curled into the sharp gravel as she struggled to keep her balance.

It was about one a.m., and the gibbous moon had not yet set. The fact that he hadn't blindfolded her only reinforced her certainty that she wouldn't live out the night. Clearly he wasn't worried about being identified.

For the first time, she faced her captor, a darker shadow among a landscape of shadows. Cool moonlight hinted at a face of strong planes and angles. What her eyes failed to register, her other senses made up for. The waves of body heat radiating from him carried his masculine scent—one part healthy, vigorous male, two parts arrogance.

The shadow form loomed larger...closer. She heard him remove his gloves; they sailed past her to land on the roof of the vehicle. Her bound legs wobbled, threatening to spill her into the gravel. His low voice broke the silence.

"You have any more surprises for me, Lizzie?"

Suddenly his hands were on her. Sliding over her hips and under the waistband of her skirt. Around her midriff and up her sides to her armpits. All the places a gun might be concealed, in a hidden pocket or holster. As brisk and impersonal as this search was, there was a shocking intimacy to it that Elizabeth couldn't ignore. She felt violated. How would she be able to stand...whatever else he had in mind?

Finally he yanked her tie-dyed blouse out of her skirt and reached under it. She held her breath and squeezed her eyes shut for the few seconds it took him to ascertain there was no small firearm tucked into her cleavage, no holster attached to her bra—convenient hiding places for an ample-breasted woman like Elizabeth Lancaster.

A sob tore through her chest as she tried to compose herself. Hysteria wouldn't solve anything, but dammit, *she didn't want to die!* Damn David for doing this to her. And damn *her* for not being able to ignore his final, terrified plea for help.

She opened her eyes and sensed her captor watching her. He was close, but not touching her. Tears streamed down her face as she wept convulsively. His dim, moonlit visage seemed to shift subtly. She almost missed his quiet words.

"Don't do that."

Her confusion must have registered. Slowly he lifted a hand to her face. The rough pad of his thumb swiped at her tears as he said, "Don't cry. You have to breathe through your nose. The tape's not coming off." His tone was subdued, matter-of-fact.

The hand left her face and came back with a tissue, which he held to her nose. "Blow."

The shock of this command was enough to stop her tears cold. That and the need to breathe. "Blow," he repeated, and she did. He wiped her nose as if she were a toddler and dropped the tissue.

She supposed it wasn't hard to make the leap from kidnapper, rapist and murderer to full-fledged litterbug.

He opened the rear door of the vehicle, then lifted her into his arms and laid her on the cold back seat, on her side facing the front. Elizabeth closed her eyes against the harsh interior car lights and kept them closed, afraid to look her attacker in the eye. He latched the seat belts snugly around her shoulders and hips, then tossed a light blanket over her, covering her from head to foot.

In moments they were moving, to the accompaniment of gravel ricocheting around the undercarriage, followed by the lulling hum of smooth asphalt as they got on the highway. She could tell he was keeping under the speed limit. No point getting stopped in the middle of a felony, even if your back-seat baggage looked like nothing more incriminating than a pile of laundry.

After a few minutes her abductor reached back and briefly slipped his hand under the blanket at her head. He touched her face lightly and slid his knuckles under her nose, obviously to make sure she was still breathing. His fingers smelled faintly of glove leather.

Eventually she felt her ear pressure change and knew they were rising in elevation. Considering New York State's wealth of mountainous terrain, that alone didn't provide a clue as to what direction they were heading.

She wondered whether Lugh had given specific instructions or had left the details of her disposal to his hired thug. At the very least, he must have demanded it happen far away. After David, it wouldn't do to have any more corpses popping up at Avalon.

Finally, after what felt like two hours, the vehicle rolled to a stop. Car doors opened and closed. Again Elizabeth squeezed her eyes shut as he hauled her out into the cool night air and slung her over his shoulder.

He unlocked a door and made his way through rooms in the dark. She could just make out plank flooring and a braided rug before he carried her up a flight of stairs and down a long hall. Abruptly he flipped her off his shoulder. She braced herself and landed hard on a bed, the wind forced from her lungs with a grunt. She blinked at the surrounding shadows, only to snap her eyes shut when he reached to the night table and flicked on a lamp.

Tremors racked her during the long silence that followed. A silence he broke with the commandment, "Open your eyes, Lizzie."

She forced herself to obey, but averted her face, staring at the cream-colored wall next to the bed. She felt his fingers on her chin, forcing her to finally look at him.

Silver eyes skewered her. It was a gaze devoid of warmth...or hope. She tried to swallow the hard knot of terror threatening to close her throat. Moonlight had only hinted at the intensity of his features—a strong, straight nose; firm, whisker-studded jaw; a wide, full mouth set in a forbidding line. His thick, light brown hair was sun-streaked and nearly brushed his shoulders. It was pushed straight back off his face, revealing a long scar on his temple. He appeared to be in his mid-thirties, about a decade older than she.

A niggling sense of recognition made her nape prickle. There was something disturbingly familiar about this man. Was it the eyes? She was sure she'd never met him before, despite his use of her name. God knew she'd have remembered.

He scrutinized her with equal intensity, that cold, unforgiving gaze burning into hers. There was no mistaking his hatred; she could almost touch it. Hatred and disgust, tempered by a hint of resignation as he unhooked a large jackknife from his belt.

Numbly Elizabeth watched the blade flip into view. *I'm going to die now.* That fact rushed to her gut with sickening force, obliterating all else. Without a thought to pride, she screamed and sobbed behind the tape and shook her head frantically, pleading with tear-filled eyes.

Don't kill me. Please. Don't do this!

Her response seemed to catch him off guard, before he blinked with sudden comprehension and some other, unidentifiable emotion. Just for an instant she saw something close to...remorse?

Then grim resolution returned as he tossed her skirt above her knees and slit the tape binding her ankles and legs.

She'd barely absorbed this latest development before he reached up and ripped the tape off her mouth. She screeched and bit her lip against the stinging pain. *"You son of a—"*

He started to retape her mouth and she shrank back, clamping her lips shut. A little lesson in who's in charge. Brusquely he rolled her onto her side and unlocked the handcuffs.

Slowly Elizabeth pulled her stiff, sore arms in front of her and massaged her reddened wrists. She hazarded a glance over her shoulder. He stood there with his arms crossed over his chest, staring at her. With trembling, half-numb fingers she managed to pull the rest of the tape off, vowing, if she lived through this night, never to have her legs waxed. At last she sat facing him, hugging her knees to her chest.

The fierce expression was back as he folded the knife against his palm. "Don't think I wasn't tempted," he said as he hooked it back on his belt.

"What—what are you going to do to me?" she asked, trying to keep her voice from quavering.

He didn't answer, just crossed to a corner occupied by a few open cardboard boxes. He hefted one of them and dumped the contents on the floor. After a few seconds, Elizabeth's jaw dropped.

"My clothes!"

The big man pawed through her things and selected a nightgown. He tossed it at her. "Put this on."

She crushed the yellow silk in her fingers to keep them from shaking. "Who are you?"

He loomed over her. "You gonna do it by yourself or do you need some help?"

Those were her storage boxes in the corner—she recognized them now. The boxes she'd left in her landlord's basement, after giving up the little apartment she'd rented in his Brooklyn home for the last three years. Her heart drummed painfully. "How did you get this stuff?"

The man took a step closer. "I told you to—"

"What did you do to Hal?" Fear for her elderly landlord made her reckless.

Her captor stared at her analytically, as if she were a specimen to be studied. Finally he said, "I doubt the old man even knows all this crap is missing. Now, I'm not a patient sort when I'm in a *good* mood. I'll give you precisely thirty seconds to change into that thing, or I'm going to do it for you."

When she could find her voice, she said, "Well, give me some privacy."

"No. You gave up the right to privacy when I found

this." He drew her semiautomatic out of his pocket and examined it with maddening casualness, ejecting the magazine, racking the slide and peering into the chamber. "I'd say it's a better-than-even chance you've got more surprises up your sleeve." He treated her to a slow once-over, concentrating on her chest. "Or somewhere. A little penknife, perhaps?"

He must know her bra contained nothing but *her*, after the way he'd groped her. She swallowed hard and licked her bloodless lips. "I...can't. I can't get undressed with you watching me."

"Touching modesty for a girl who spent the last three weeks playing house with Lugh," he sneered, correctly pronouncing the name *Loo.*

"It wasn't like that."

"Save it. You think I don't know what goes on at the Avalon Collective? It isn't all peace, love and compost, sweetheart. Well, maybe it is for most of the poor chumps who end up there. But not for your esteemed leader, am I right?"

He was right, damn it.

He continued, "As I understand it, Lugh has more...compelling needs. Needs that can only be met by the more nubile members of the commune."

"Not me. I didn't do that."

He snorted in disbelief. "Yeah, right. A hot piece like you? My guess is you've been keeping the guy's bed warm since the day you joined. So do us both a favor and drop the quivering-virgin routine." He slipped her gun back in his pocket. "Your dubious acting ability is wasted on me. You're just not believable as a blushing ingenue. Stick to those late-night phone-sex commercials—that's more your speed. What is it...one-nine-hundred-*JIGGLE*?"

She repressed a groan of embarrassment. So he'd caught those sleazy 1-900 commercials. That was sure to elevate her credibility!

Lord, how she'd despised that role—purring into a foggy camera lens while caressing a phone receiver. She'd resisted auditioning for the part, but eventually extreme financial desperation and her agent's hectoring had won out. Acting jobs were scarce, and Elizabeth had rent to pay. And it was only commercials, after all—she would never actually work for a phone-sex business.

Of course, this hateful creep knew that. His point was merely to add insult to enormous injury. But how did he know so much about her? And why did he talk about Lugh—the former Graham Hoyt-Gaines turned commune leader—as if he weren't the man's hireling? If he wasn't working for Lugh, then why had he...

Her captor closed the distance between them and lifted the nightgown from her stiff fingers. His voice was as smooth as the silk he caressed. "Then again, maybe you *want* me to undress you. Is that why you're dawdling, Lizzie? So I'll get impatient and—"

She lurched to her knees and snatched the gown out of his hands. "Go to hell!" Her temples throbbed with the force of her sudden fury. "You're a goddamn bully! Does it get you *hot* to terrorize a helpless woman? *Does it?* Maybe that's the only way you can—" She stopped abruptly, her heart slamming, her heaving breaths like fire in her chest. "And don't call me Lizzie," she rasped. "I hate it."

Her little tirade left him if not speechless, at least subdued. A strange disquiet lurked behind those icy silver eyes now, as if he'd just completed a jigsaw puzzle, only to find a leftover piece that had no slot. He said, "I thought everyone called you Lizzie."

She drew in a quick breath. Not *everyone*.

But whoever sicced this maniac on her must have.

"I prefer to be called Elizabeth." Not that anyone had ever given a damn about her preferences. She dragged her fingers through her disheveled hair, pushing it off her face. She felt deflated, drained. "Can't you just turn around while I change?"

The lines of his face hardened. "No. You could be hiding a—"

"I'm not! I swear." She spread her arms wide as if to demonstrate the truth of her words. "That gun was all I had."

"I didn't realize Lugh was arming his people. What is it, a little nineties paranoid survivalism mixed in with the sixties warm-and-fuzzy crap? Lemme ask you, do you even know how to *use* that thing?"

She sighed raggedly. "Look. You *know* I don't have any other weapons. You've searched me thoroughly." She still felt the imprint of his hands on her body.

He laughed. "Sweetheart, if you think *that* was a thorough search, you don't have much of an imagination. I'd be happy to demonstrate precisely how *thorough* a search can be."

His words hit her like a pail of cold water. She

wouldn't put it past him. Her eyes stung. She swallowed the tears clogging her throat and dropped her gaze to the buttons of her blouse. And watched her frigid fingers rise mechanically to slip a button through a buttonhole. And tried to pretend this was happening to someone else. Another button free. And another.

A low, raw oath broke her concentration. She looked up to see her abductor's broad back. "You have thirty seconds," he growled, and made a show of checking his watch. "Starting now."

Twenty-nine seconds later she pulled the gown down over her knees as he turned to face her. She used to love this old-fashioned, sleeveless nightie, made of heavy, slippery satin with delicate lace detail on the fitted, low-cut bodice. This gown used to make her feel pretty. Now it just made her feel more wretchedly vulnerable.

She forced herself to sit primly on the edge of the bed with her hands folded in her lap. He was looking at her. She stared straight ahead at an antique, marble-topped washstand. Her breasts pushed against the silk, and every breath reminded her how well she filled out this gown.

He stepped closer and she held her breath, but he merely lifted her tie-dyed blouse and long skirt—regulation garments for female members of Avalon—and the decidedly nonregulation neoprene thigh holster connected to a supporting waist strap.

"I'm going to burn all this," he said, rolling the clothes into a bundle. "From now on, you wear only your normal stuff." He indicated the mound of clothing on the floor.

From now on...? There was going to be a from now on?

She held his ruthless stare as she came to her feet. She'd been kidnapped. Pawed. Humiliated. Known terror beyond anything she'd ever experienced. It was time for some answers. In slow, modulated tones she muttered, "Who are you, and what the hell is going on here?"

"We'll talk tomorrow. Get back on the bed."

She looked at the double bed. And at him. His sneer of distaste answered her unvoiced fear.

"Don't worry, sweetheart," he said. "I figure you're due for a rest."

Rationally she was grateful he considered her too sullied to consort with, but that didn't keep her from feeling small and cheap under his condemning stare.

"Come on," he said, pushing none too gently on her shoulders till she fell back on the bed. "There's time for a couple hours of shut-eye before reveille." He tucked her clothes under his arm and lifted the handcuffs from the night table.

"No!" She tried to rise, but he pushed her down easily and seized her left wrist, shackling it to the decorative, wrought-iron headboard. "You don't have to use these," she argued. "I'm not going anywhere."

"No kidding." He dragged the bedcovers over her, tucking her in like a child. "I'll be right next door." He turned off the lamp and started to leave. He paused in the doorway, his teeth gleaming in the dark. "And I'm a light sleeper, Lizzie."

Then she was alone. With nothing but her disordered thoughts for company.

Lizzie. Only one other person insisted on calling her that even when she asked him not to. But David couldn't have any connection with this psychopath.

David was dead.

She hadn't even been allowed to go to the funeral. She'd gotten that phone call...

That horrible phone call. Asking her—no, *ordering* her—to stay away from the church and the cemetery. *You've done enough damage. The family doesn't want you there.* That disembodied voice had haunted her for weeks, till she'd half believed the ugly accusation.

He's dead because of you.

Elizabeth stopped breathing.

That voice!

She lurched up, only to be jerked back down by the handcuffs.

She was right—she *had* seen those eyes before. In photographs, anyway. Her mouth went dry. Perhaps she'd been better off not knowing. Now only one question remained.

What was the mighty commando going to do to her?

2

HE COULD TELL AT ONCE that she hadn't slept. Those big brown eyes were puffy and red rimmed, and she had that jumpy, unfocused look of deep exhaustion.

Good. He hoped she'd spent the last few hours agonizing over her plight, wondering who this monster was who held her at his mercy. Her hoarse greeting dashed those fond hopes.

"Good morning, Caleb."

He paused in the act of unlocking the handcuffs. Well, there was one source of amusement gone. David's little play toy was just full of surprises.

"Morning, Lizzie." He *might* accede to her wishes and call her Elizabeth. Perhaps while ice-skating in Hades. "Sleep well?"

"I had more pleasant ways to occupy my time. Like calculating the prison sentence for kidnapping." She drew her left arm down and cradled it against her chest, wincing slightly.

He curled his fingers around the handcuffs to keep from reaching to soothe the raw abrasions on her left wrist. If he found it hard to summon the ruthlessness he needed to deal with Lizzie Lancaster, all he had to do was remember what she'd done to his brother.

She said, "You're out of uniform, Rambo." Her eyes

were hard and glittering. He saw that at some point during the wee hours, raw loathing had replaced her previous terror. That was fine with him.

He knew she must be trying to figure out a way to get at her weapon. That's what *he'd* be doing. "Don't even consider it," he said. "This whole place has been Lizzie-proofed. You won't find a knife anywhere. Nothing made of glass. Ditto for heavy, blunt objects. Of course, you *could* try to strangle me with a lamp cord. That would be mildly entertaining."

Staring down at her, he laid out the options. "It's up to you how we play this, sweetheart. Personally, I'm not one for the traditional, heavy-handed approach. Nonstop interrogation. Bondage. Threats. No sleep. No privacy. That way is quick, but brutal, and creates more problems than it solves, if you ask me."

He saw comprehension dawn, and almost laughed at her expression of stunned disbelief. She sat bolt upright in the bed. "You're trying to deprogram me!" With her glossy brown hair in disarray and lively color flooding her face and throat—and those magnificent full breasts straining her gown with each agitated breath—she looked like a vision out of a teenager's wet dream. At that moment he couldn't blame his brother for losing his head over this woman.

He said, "Took you long enough to catch on. Now, I'm sure Lugh has filled your head with horror stories about deprogramming. And you know what?" He grinned. "They're all true! It's not something you want to experience. Take my word for it."

She groaned. "I don't believe this."

"Lucky for you, I'm a civilized fellow. I prefer to hold off on the rough stuff and just sit back and give you a chance to come to your senses. It'll take time, but hey—" he shrugged "—I've got time. It all depends on you, Lizzie. On whether you behave yourself."

"Behave myself!"

"Cooperate and we'll do this the low-impact, hands-off way. Plenty of satisfying quality time for you and me, discussing the finer points of your incredibly moronic and self-destructive decision to join Lugh's commune. Who knows? You might even end up thanking me."

Her expression said, *Don't hold your breath.*

"Of course, if you choose to fight me—or try to escape—we do this the old-fashioned way." He dangled the handcuffs over her. "Easy for me. Not too fun for you. Think about it."

She threw off the covers and stood up. She was tall for a woman—five eight or nine—but of course, he still towered over her.

"Who'd hire a deprogrammer to go after *me*?" she demanded. "I didn't tell anyone I was joining the Avalon Collective. And even if I did, there's not a soul alive who'd give a damn."

A muscle in his jaw twitched. "You're right about that, Lizzie," he said coldly. "The soul in question is very much dead."

He saw it sink in. Saw her eyes cloud with pain before she averted them. She took a deep breath and said, "David would never have asked you to do something like this to me."

"Why?" Caleb sneered. "Because he loved you too much?"

She met his eyes again, her own glazed with grief or guilt—he didn't know which, and right then, he didn't much care. "Yes," she said quietly.

He gripped the handcuffs so hard that pain shot through his fingers. "He died loving you, Lizzie. After everything you did to him. How does that make you feel?" He took a step toward her, crowding her, but she stood her ground. "Does it give you some kind of warped thrill to string men along, make them think you care—"

"Is that what he told you?"

He held up his palm to silence her. Strove for control. "You don't want to have this conversation, sweetheart. Trust me. This is as good as my mood's gonna get around you, and it won't take much to put me over the edge."

Her features tightened in frustration. He could tell she was dying to spout her little lies and evasions—all those rationalizations she must have spent the last few months cooking up to justify her heartless treatment of a man who'd loved her to distraction...and ultimately couldn't live without her.

To Caleb's surprise, she simply asked, "How does David fit into all this?"

"First off, let me assure you that if it was up to me, I'd have gladly let you vegetate in that damn commune, and good riddance. Hell, in your case, a little brainwashing can only be an improvement."

She just stared silently.

He said, "But David called me, right before he died. Swore me to a vow. 'Lizzie's got no family,' he said, 'no one to keep her safe.' He made me promise to look after you if something happened to him."

Good Lord. "And you went along with this?"

"I was just trying to calm him down. How was I to know he was planning to hang himself..."

"And force you to make good on your promise."

"He was so rattled, I'd have agreed to anything. I tried to talk some sense into him, get him to come home, but he said there was something he had to do." His voice turned steely. "And we know what that turned out to be."

Caleb clenched his jaw, remembering David's irrational rambling, his unstable state of mind during that last conversation. His younger brother had always been emotionally immature, but after Lizzie's brutal rejection, he'd spun out of control, lost his grip on reality. That's when he'd thrown in his lot with the Avalon Collective—not exactly a hotbed of stable, balanced individuals. David hadn't a prayer of getting his head straight among those tie-dyed misfits.

When he'd first learned of David's death, Caleb had briefly considered the possibility of foul play. Once he'd calmed down and thought it through, however, he was forced to face the truth.

Obviously David had joined Avalon in a desperate bid to put his blighted relationship with Lizzie behind him, to start over and try to find some purpose in life. Unfortunately, the damage had already been done. *Depressed* was too benign a term for David's state of mind during that last conversation. Hadn't he warned Caleb then of his intentions? When he made him promise to look after Lizzie "if something happened" to him?

Caleb refused to delude himself. All the evidence pointed to suicide. The only foul play involved was the more subtle brand dished out by Lizzie Lancaster. She alone was responsible for David's misery and his final act of self-destruction.

"Caleb," she said with surprising gentleness, "why didn't you do this to *him?*" She indicated herself, the room, the jumble of her meager possessions in the corner. "Why didn't you just go in and get him out?"

His chest expanded on a deep, shuddering breath, culminating in a grim chuckle; if he didn't laugh, he'd cry. "Because kidnapping's against the law. It seemed like too extreme a solution at the time. I kept telling myself he'd…snap out of it."

But he hadn't. And then it was too late. The terrible irony was that getting David out of there was precisely the kind of mission Caleb had been trained for as a Special Forces operative. And he was one of the best. But when it came to saving his own brother…

He'd failed.

Lizzie hugged herself. She looked him in the eye. "If David asked you to look after me, he couldn't have meant…" She shook her head, trembling, as if denying the events of the last few hours. "I can take care of myself. I absolve you of any responsibility for me."

"It doesn't work that way. I made a solemn vow to my brother, Lizzie. My little brother, who's dead now because of you. God knows you're not worth an iota of my time or trouble—any more than you were worth the pathetic adoration he heaped on you—but that's beside the point. I promised to keep you out of danger, and that meant getting you out of that commune. And deprogramming you so you'd stay out. Maybe you wouldn't end up offing yourself like David did, but there are plenty of other dangers there. Drugs, no doubt. And you ever hear of AIDS?"

"You've got it wrong, Caleb. I'm not a member of Avalon, not really." At his bark of laughter she said, "Listen to me! The only reason I joined was to look into David's death. I think he—"

Caleb grabbed her by the shoulders and roughly turned her around, dragging down the wide strap of her nightgown. There it was, on her right shoulder blade. A tiny tattoo of the sun, the obligatory brand for members of the Avalon Collective. The leader, an Englishman named Graham Hoyt-Gaines, had renamed himself Lugh after the ancient Celtic sun god.

Lizzie clutched the gown to keep it from sliding down. "Let me explain—"

"Shut up! Save your lies for some lovestruck sap like my brother." Caleb caressed the little tattoo and felt a deep shiver ripple through her. She jerked away from his hands and pulled the strap back up her shoulder. When she faced him, her expression was venomous.

He said, "In the laughably unlikely event that you're telling the truth, that puts you in even greater danger. Did you think of that? Sneaking around Avalon, snooping into God knows what. All the more reason for me to step in and honor my vow." He could tell by her expression that, indeed, she hadn't thought her ridiculous story through to this logical conclusion.

"Face it, Lizzie. We're stuck with each other. At least until you can convince me you're ready to turn your back on that mind-melting commune and go back to being the same sweet, loving gal you were before," he said with blistering sarcasm. "And you'd better make it one of your better performances, sweetheart, 'cause you're starting out with a few strikes against you in the trust department."

She stiffened her spine, raised her chin. "If you let me go right now, I'll forget this happened. But I swear to God, Caleb, if you continue to keep me here against my will, I won't rest till you're behind bars."

Her threats meant nothing. He had no intention of releasing her until he was one hundred percent convinced she'd been successfully deprogrammed. And by then she'd be grateful for his intervention, not looking to turn him in.

He nodded at the boxes and heap of clothing on the floor. "Stow all your gear and get your fanny down to the kitchen by 0700." He looked at his watch. "That's twenty minutes from now. You're going to do your share of cooking and cleaning around here."

One dark eyebrow rose. "Right. You kidnap me and hold me prisoner, and then expect me to play housewife? In your dreams, Rambo."

He shrugged. "The choice is yours. No work, no food." He jangled the handcuffs. "And no freedom."

She held his stare for long moments, as if debating further argument. Then she walked around him to the boxes. She glanced in each one, grimacing at the disordered jumble. She'd left everything neatly packed.

"I confiscated a few items," he informed her.

"Let me guess. Knives, glassware and heavy blunt objects," she said dryly. She was scanning the room for something.

"You're catching on. See? We're going to get along just fine."

He'd made it to the doorway when she asked, "Where's my medication?"

Medication? Caleb frowned. What kind of...

Then it hit him and he burst out laughing. Clever girl. Invent the right kind of medical problem and he'd *have* to release her. "You almost had me going there for a second. Maybe I underestimated your acting skills..." His words trailed off as he watched the color leach from her face. Just how good an actress was she?

She plopped heavily onto the edge of the bed and slumped with her head in her hands. "It was in my room. At Avalon. Did you get the stuff from my room?"

"Sweetheart, I didn't show up there with a moving van. The only piece of baggage I was interested in was in the latrine, scouring toilets."

At one a.m. Every night, after a full day of chores. If he hadn't snatched her, they probably would have worked her to death.

Lizzie surprised him. Now that he'd actually met

the object of his surveillance face-to-face, he couldn't help wondering what would drive a woman like this to join Avalon. She had guts; he'd give her that. And she was sharp. Sure as hell didn't fit his image of a wit-less commune cutie.

He said, "A piece of advice, Lizzie. You and I will get along a lot better once you give up these little cha-rades and start playing straight with me."

He started out the doorway, but for some reason his hand caught the frame and wouldn't let him leave. He stood there cursing himself before finally turning back to her.

"Okay," he said disgustedly. "I'll bite. What kind of medication?"

"A beta-blocker. I have to take it every day."

"A *beta-blocker*? Isn't that for heart conditions?"

"In my case, I take it to help prevent migraines."

He breathed a silent sigh of relief. "So all we're talk-ing about here is headaches."

She stared at him, her expression bleak. "What we're talking about here are blinding, crippling mi-graines. Calling it a headache is like calling a bleeding ulcer indigestion. I have two other medications be-sides that—one to stop the migraine when it's just starting and a heavy-duty painkiller for when the other two fail." Those enormous eyes widened with hope. "You could get the prescriptions filled. My doc-tor's number—"

"Forget it. The last thing I want is for you to get comfortably settled in here for the long haul. Once I'm sure of a genuine attitude adjustment, you're outta here. If you happen to suffer in the process...well, hey, that's just an added bonus for me."

If he'd slapped her, she couldn't have looked more wounded...more vulnerable. Caleb felt like something scraped off the bottom of a shoe. Laboriously he dredged up memories of David, and what Lizzie had done to him. For some reason, it wasn't enough this time, and Caleb had to struggle to shore up his resolve.

With visible effort she composed herself. She rose and crossed to the lowboy dresser. Began picking up items of clothing, folding them and placing them in the empty drawers.

"Twenty minutes, Lizzie," he reminded her, and left her to her task.

ELIZABETH PICKED HER WAY along the leaf-strewn path until the woods thinned and gave way to the lawn surrounding the Trent family home. Her prison.

David had told her that when the boys' father died twenty-six years ago, their mother had sold their magnificent apartment on Central Park South in Manhattan and taken up permanent residence in what had been their summer home in upstate New York. A paranoid recluse, she'd had razor wire installed atop the high stone fence enclosing this wooded, twenty-acre estate in the Adirondacks, and had never stepped outside the gate.

So where was she now? Elizabeth and Caleb were the only inhabitants of this sprawling, two-story log home, a monument to rustic opulence. The razor wire was still intact, and after walking the perimeter of the grounds, straining her ears in vain for sounds of human activity, Elizabeth understood how truly isolated she was. She could scream herself hoarse for days on end and no one would hear.

She'd endured a strained breakfast and lunch, during which the topic of conversation was limited to Lugh and the Avalon Collective. Nerves kept her stomach knotted, and she barely touched her food. But she did assist, as ordered, in meal preparation and cleanup.

The rest of the day had been her own. Apparently as long as she did as she was told and didn't get belligerent, her captor was willing to grant her the time and privacy needed to "come to her senses."

And she did plan to cooperate, having decided to play along for the time being. After all, what choice did she have? She couldn't hope to overpower him. If she was going to escape, it would have to be through her wits.

Her informal tour had confirmed that he had indeed removed all potentially dangerous objects from the house and grounds. The kitchen was stocked with paper and plastic. Caleb used that big pocketknife of his on whatever needed to be chopped. Not a heavy cast-iron pan in sight. No razors or pharmaceuticals in the medicine chests. She'd found empty phone jacks in several rooms.

The toolshed and garage were kept locked, as well as a room in the finished basement and another off the kitchen. He held the keys to every room in the house.

Worse than the knowledge that he could lock her *in* any room was the fact that she couldn't lock him *out*. As a consequence, she'd kept one eye on the bathroom door while she showered that morning.

Caleb had retreated to his first-floor study after breakfast and lunch, busy with some kind of paperwork. With that insulting arrogance of his, he'd invited her to make herself at home, explore the house and grounds...practically *begged* her to search for a means of escape, so confident was he that she'd come up empty-handed.

Smiling to herself, she blessed his overconfidence. Left to her own devices, she'd quietly opened a trapdoor in the second-floor ceiling and pulled down a ladder leading to the stuffy attic. Among the old furniture, clothing and toys stored there, she'd made an intriguing discovery. And hatched a plan she prayed would work.

The sun was dipping toward the western horizon and a cool breeze was picking up. She shoved her hands into the pockets of her ratty old windbreaker and rounded the house. And stopped short when she saw Caleb squatting near the back porch. He hadn't noticed her; his attention was fixed on the scrawny cat he was petting. Even from a distance she discerned the cat's incongruously plump belly, heavy with a litter of kittens.

He was running his big hand over her black fur and crooning to her as she leaned into the caress. A warm half smile softened his features. Elizabeth was struck by the memory of his callused thumb wiping at her tears the night before, as she stood bound and terrified, propped against his Land Rover. It was the only time his touch had been gentle. Somehow the realization that he was capable of tenderness unsettled her more than the brutal treatment she'd endured at his hands.

The cat, obviously homeless, yowled insistently, and Caleb didn't disappoint it. Elizabeth shook her head and smiled knowingly when he produced a can of tuna. The instant the can opener punched through the lid and the cat got a whiff of the contents, it began rubbing against him in a frenzy of feline gratitude and anticipation, nearly nudging the can out of his hands. It attacked its dinner while he was still scraping it into a small plastic bowl.

For a while he simply watched her eat. And Elizabeth watched him. Watched the subtle shift and flex of powerful muscles under the cream-colored cable-knit sweater and blue jeans. Every movement he made, no matter how slight, reminded her of his extraordinary strength. And of her helplessness.

When Caleb tried to pet the cat while it ate, it dismissed him with an irritated flick of its tail. He looked up when Elizabeth approached. His expression lost some of its softness and became flatter somehow.

His silver gaze flicked over her threadbare jacket, with its frayed cuffs and broken zipper, to her faded leggings and battered sneakers. His expression never changed, but still she cringed inwardly. She cursed her foolish embarrassment. Caleb had pawed through her things, after all. He already knew how shabby her clothes were, how cheap and dilapidated her other possessions. Even her beloved, vintage silk night-gowns were thrift-shop finds!

She cleared her throat and tried to smile. "Don't you know what they say? Once you feed a stray, you're stuck with it."

He stared at her pointedly and said, "Let's hope they were wrong."

Her fingers tightened into fists inside her pockets. Was this SOB determined to turn everything into an insult? She opened her mouth to ask him just that, then closed it and slid her gaze to the cat. She had nothing to gain by further antagonizing him.

And everything to gain by lulling him into a false sense of complacency.

The cat had scarfed down the tuna and now sat cleaning its face and paws. Caleb stood up. "I just didn't want the damn thing keeling over on my prop-erty," he said gruffly. "She won't stick around. Cats are independent. Now that she's gotten what she was after, she'll go bother someone else."

Elizabeth bit her lip. *And give up fancy albacore? A pregnant, half-starved cat? If you say so, Rambo.*

She said, "I thought your mother lived here."

"My mother died shortly after David did."

"Oh, Caleb. I'm so sorry." The heartfelt words were out before she realized it.

"The shock of losing David was too much for her. The strain on her heart..."

His cold stare was brutally eloquent. With a sick jolt Elizabeth realized he blamed her for his mother's death as well. But Madeleine Trent's health had been declining for some time, according to David. Surely Caleb must have known that, even if he only made it home on infrequent leaves.

That thought spawned a glimmer of hope. Elizabeth asked, "Are you on furlough?" Perhaps he'd have to report back to service soon.

"I quit the army."

His words stunned her. He *quit*? David's hotshot commando brother was now a...civilian?

She recalled the two photos she'd seen, the ones that had triggered her recognition of him. One was a framed formal portrait David kept on his mantel, of Caleb in his dress uniform, complete with a beret sporting some mysterious insignia. She was told he'd attended West Point and distinguished himself in the Green Berets before being recruited for the Delta Force, the army's elite counterterrorist and assault unit. He'd attained the rank of captain.

David had borne little resemblance to the face in that portrait, with its sensual, unsmiling mouth and pale, penetrating eyes. Caleb was older than David by eight years, his rugged features seasoned by the kind of life his brother, a graphic artist in Manhattan, could only imagine.

The other picture was a snapshot David had carried in his wallet. Caleb outdoors somewhere, grinning into the camera, wearing camouflage utilities and a matching bush hat...and loosely carrying some sort of evil-looking weapon. That man was much more intriguing than the stiffly handsome officer in the formal portrait. *Here* was the flesh-and-blood commando.

"What kinds of missions does he go on?" she'd asked David.

"He doesn't like to talk about it," he'd answered.

She asked now, "Why did you quit?" Caleb's expression told her she had no business asking. "Didn't mean to be impertinent," she added dryly. "Is it all right to ask what you do nowadays?" Not that he needed to work to keep the wolf from the door—the Trents were loaded. But somehow she couldn't imagine this man living a life of idle leisure.

"I'm a freelance security consultant. That's what I was working on today—a couple of proposals."

"So in other words, people hire you to tell them how to keep the bad guys from doing what you did last night."

She could have sworn he was fighting a smile. He reached down to pet the cat, but it sprang away and darted across the lawn. He asked, "Where were you just now?"

"The woods."

He looked at her sharply. "I don't want you in there unless I'm with you."

"You gonna protect me from the lions and tigers and bears? Oh my."

He eyed her loose windbreaker. "You'd be surprised what kinds of weapons can be fashioned from things you find in the woods."

"They teach you that stuff in Rambo school?"

Casually he reached for the open front of her jacket, and without warning, something inside her snapped.

"No!" She backed away, as quivering rage surged through every cell of her body. "You are not putting your hands on me again," she vowed. Her fingernails gouged her palms. Quickly she scanned him from head to toe, choosing a target. By God, if he touched her, she'd smash that nice straight nose, and to hell with cooperation.

After an interminable stare-down he said, "All right. Show me, then." He crossed his arms and nodded, indicating she should open her jacket, perhaps turn out the pockets.

"Go to hell."

"I advise you to reconsider, Lizzie. It's not often I'm willing to compromise."

She dragged in a deep, calming breath. "What do you imagine I could be hiding?"

He shrugged. "A rock. A sharp stick, maybe."

"A *rock?"* She rolled her eyes and flapped the sides of her jacket. That was *her* compromise. "Satisfied, Rambo?" she sneered. "No rocks. You won't get beaned in your sleep."

His jaw worked. "Don't call me Rambo."

"Don't call me Lizzie."

When he just glared at her she laughed lightly and said, "Trust a man to fret about sticks and stones when the woods are chock-full of such *intriguing* plant life."

She paused to watch her words sink in. When his

eyes began to widen she said, "Well, I'd better get supper started," and quickly scooted past him into the house.

3

"PLEASE, GOD, let this work." Elizabeth wiped her sweaty palms on her jeans and loosened the wing nut under the little round launchpad, adjusting the angle of flight.

The three-foot launch rod had been the hardest thing to smuggle out of the attic. Everything else fit in the pockets of her loose jeans and under her jacket. Finally, in desperation, she'd slipped the rod up her sleeve and clutched a wool scarf to conceal the bottom few inches. Caleb was busy in the garage, working on his Land-Rover, so he probably hadn't even noticed her leave the house and enter the woods, but she couldn't be too careful. Hadn't he warned her what would happen if she tried to escape?

She'd spent three days playing the cooperative little captive, their interactions strained but civil. Three days trying to display the appropriate attitude adjustment, wary of Rambo's threat of the "rough stuff" that constituted traditional deprogramming. Three long days waiting for the right moment to implement the plan she'd hatched when she discovered a carton of old model-rocket parts in the attic, under a pile of worn-out sports equipment and a dusty model-railroad layout.

She fitted the launch rod into the launchpad, then pulled the nose cone and clear plastic payload bay off the foot-long rocket—a heavy cardboard tube, actually, painted blue and silver—revealing the little red-and-white plastic parachute and a long rubber band connecting the parts.

Now for the critical step. From her pocket she retrieved the note she'd written earlier, a plea for help detailing her identity and location, and inserted it into the clear payload bay, where it would be seen immediately by whoever found the rocket.

She paused to peer through the bare trees and listen intently. Not that she'd hear Caleb approach, even through the piles of dried leaves. The man moved like a phantom. Often she'd turn around and he'd just be there, with no warning. Made her jumpy as hell.

A faint sense of disorientation accompanied her intense concentration. She squeezed her eyes shut and licked her dry lips. *Don't let this happen now. Not now. Let me finish this at least.*

Pulling in a shaky breath, she drew the battered instruction sheet out of her pocket and scanned it again, then quickly assembled the rocket, securing its engine and slipping it onto the launch rod. Alligator clips connected the wire igniter to seventeen feet of insulated cord and the rectangular, plastic launch controller. She'd had to scrounge up four *AA* batteries for the controller. She hoped to be rescued before Caleb tried to use his miniflashlight or TV remote control.

She carried the controller out of the small clearing into the trees. Inserted the safety key and watched the signal light go on. Said a quick prayer and pushed the launch button.

The rocket shot over the stone wall with a hissing whoosh and a trail of white smoke. In awe she watched it soar over the treetops, before it separated and the parachute deployed, about a quarter mile away.

Yes! She'd done it! Fervently she prayed it hadn't become snagged on a high treetop. Or landed in one of the myriad lakes dotting the Adirondacks. Or...

No. She couldn't think that way. This had to work.

The smell of sulfur overpowered the dry, earthy scents of autumn growth and decay. Quickly she shoved the launch apparatus under some shrubbery, covered it with leaves and trudged back through the woods.

The disorientation persisted, the telltale "aura" she'd come to recognize and dread. She had no doubt the stress of the last hour was a contributing factor. Not to mention her unmedicated state.

As the house came into view she automatically glanced toward the detached two-car garage. Through the open door she saw Caleb's dark green Land Rover and his mother's ancient, little-used, black Lincoln Continental.

But no Caleb.

Elizabeth stopped dead in her tracks. Her pulse kicked into high gear and she felt the first tentative jabs of that hot poker over her left eye. Slowly her gaze swept back to the house, where she thought she saw a hint of movement in the attic window.

The hot poker danced to a throbbing beat and she snapped her eyes shut. Then pried them open to look at the attic window again. She saw the wavering reflection of gently drifting clouds, stained salmon by the westering sun...the shadow of a naked tree limb twitching in the stiff breeze. She swallowed hard and mentally scolded herself. *This is not a good time to panic, Elizabeth.*

Approaching the back door, she noticed a small bowl on the ground, begrimed with a few flecks of dry tuna.

God, it even hurt to smile.

CALEB CHARGED into her bedroom without knocking, and was surprised to find the room nearly dark. She'd drawn the drapes, but he was able to make out her form curled up on the bed.

"No rest for the wicked!" he bellowed, flicking on the light.

She moaned and curled up tighter, pressing her arms over her eyes. He crossed the room and tossed the handcuffs onto the night table with a loud clatter. She flinched at the noise.

"Knock it off, Lizzie. I know you're awake. You just came in the house." He gave her a bone-jangling shake.

Something about the frantic way she shrieked, "Don't!" made him stop. "The light," she groaned. "Turn it off...."

The *light?* He didn't want to know what kind of stunt she was cooking up now.

For three days he'd watched her pretend to play by his rules. Not that he'd trusted her for an instant. Still, how could he have known that her move, when she made it, would be so spectacularly resourceful? He felt like an idiot for letting it happen. He'd underestimated her.

Well, she'd given him a good lesson in humility, but now it was time to dispense a lesson of his own. He wrenched her arms from her face and pushed her onto her back, pinning her to the bed. Her eyes were clamped shut, and the left one was tearing.

She nearly had him buying it, too, before he remembered he was dealing with a professional actress. And he knew damn well those sleazy phone-sex commercials constituted only the hungry dregs of her career. Lizzie had done some respectable work in commercials and legitimate theater. Nothing electrifying, but she'd managed to keep a roof over her head for four years in New York. He couldn't deny a grudging respect.

And now Sarah Bernhardt was turning those vaunted talents his way. He shook her again, roughly, and she cried out.

"Caleb...please," she whispered, as if even speaking was painful. Her eyes never opened. "It's a migraine. A bad one. The light..."

"What convenient timing, sweetheart," he scoffed, but he released her. Could a migraine come on that fast?

Slowly she rolled upright and sat pressing her fingers over her left eye. "Gotta get ice," she murmured.

She stood up and took a wobbly step, her head down, her eyes squinted nearly shut.

Caleb reached out to steady her, feeling a bit of that welcome ire slip away. Welcome because it was protective. As long as he kept his hatred fresh, she couldn't get under his skin, the way she nearly had these past few days. He knew her track record, after all. This was the wrong damn woman to let under your skin.

With one hand on her shoulder, he lifted her chin and peered closely at her. Her face was drawn, sheened with sweat. If she was acting, she should get an Academy Award. He looked at the handcuffs and back at her. Just how ruthless was he?

She moved away from him and started toward the door.

"Get back in bed," he growled. "I'll get the ice."

When he returned, the room was dark once more. It was dusk, and little light made it through the drapes.

Her voice was small and tentative. "Caleb...?"

"I'm here, Lizzie."

She lay curled up with her back to him. When he sat on the edge of the bed, she slowly unfolded herself, like a flower, onto her back. Their hips touched. Even in the murky semidark he saw her eyes were closed. She lifted her hand and rested it on his upper arm.

It was a gesture of helplessness. Of trust. An unwelcome pressure swelled in his chest, a sensation he told himself had nothing to do with tender feelings for this woman.

Gently he placed the plastic ice bag on her forehead, and she shifted it to the left side.

"Is that where it hurts?" he asked. "On the left?"

"Yeah," she whispered. "It's like a...hot poker. It's always on that side."

In the dark he touched her face and felt the moisture sliding out of her left eye. Only that eye. He sighed in self-disgust. "Damn..."

That she was suffering couldn't be denied. That he was partly responsible, through his thoughtless indifference to her need for medication, brought an ugly little rush of shame. Despite his taunting words that first day, he'd never meant to be the instrument of her suffering.

What would David say?

Caleb stroked her cheek. Her expression was still...so still, as if it hurt even to move the muscles of her face. He smoothed his fingers over her forehead to ease the tension he felt there. She whimpered, "No," and tightened her fingers on his arm.

He dropped his hand, feeling useless. "I'll get you some aspirin."

"It won't help—" Suddenly she curled into herself, clutching her stomach. "Oh no..." The words ended on a low, desolate moan. "I'm gonna be sick!" She was already rising, holding her head.

"I've got you." He rose with her, supporting her out the door and down the hall to the bathroom. He felt the perspiration soaking through her flannel shirt, a shirt as threadbare as the rest of her things.

Not for the first time, he wondered if she'd been after David's money. Then again, if she'd gotten anything out of him, wouldn't she have *something* to show for it? Jewelry, a fur coat...? Decent clothes at the very least. Maybe there was a bank account he knew nothing about.

But then, new members of the Avalon Collective were required to turn over all their assets to the commune—every last penny. If his brother had given Lizzie anything, it was Lugh's now. David himself had obediently wiped out his generous bank accounts, stocks and bonds, and real-estate holdings. Caleb could only assume she'd done the same.

The bathroom they entered was as luxuriously rustic as the rest of the house, well appointed and spacious. His hand automatically went to the light switch, but he stopped himself. Diffuse twilight washed in through the large skylight overhead, glinting off porcelain. She dropped to her knees in front of the bowl, holding her head, breathing hard. He joined her on the floor and gathered her hair back.

"No!" she wailed. "Go away!"

"Sweetheart, I've seen folks puke before. I won't faint."

"Please..." When he didn't move, she swatted blindly at him, and he seized her wrists.

"You're pitiful, you know that?" he said. "Save your energy, Lizzie." He pulled her hair back once more, twisted it and tucked it under her collar.

"I hate you," she whimpered.

"Yes, I know you do," he said soothingly. *I'm less*

than thrilled with myself just now. He held her while her stomach emptied violently.

She sagged against him. Carefully he pulled her up, wiped her face with a cold washcloth and helped her rinse her mouth and stagger back to bed.

"Who's your doctor?" he asked, replacing the ice pack.

The arms covering her face shifted and he saw one eye blink. Or try to. "My doctor?" she croaked.

"Too little too late, I know, but..." Caleb pulled open the night-table drawer and extracted a pen and scratch pad. "What's his name and number?"

"Moira O'Neal," she said, and gave him the Brooklyn phone number.

"All right, you sit tight. I'll go call her."

He retrieved a phone from the locked storage room off the kitchen. Ten minutes after he left a message with her service, Dr. O'Neal called him back. Lizzie was on vacation upstate, he explained, and had forgotten her medication. She was having a real thumper of a migraine. The doctor instructed him to have the pharmacy call for the prescriptions, and gave him a few helpful bits of advice.

Silently he entered Lizzie's room and approached the bed. In the light spilling in from the hallway, he saw her lying very still, with one arm thrown over her eyes. His guts twisting, he lifted the handcuffs from the night table. She turned her head at the scraping sound, and he held the cuffs behind his back. *Don't think about it*, he told himself. *Just do it.*

She murmured, "Caleb..."

He bent over her and brushed his fingertips across her damp forehead and cheek. "I'm going out now," he said quietly. "The drugstore's about twenty minutes away. I'll be back as soon as I can." He paused. "You'll be okay."

Just do it. Gently he lifted her wrist and brought it to the headboard. Her eyes squinted at the handcuffs and snapped to his face. In the heartbeat of time before she averted her gaze, he read undiluted anguish, the pain of betrayal.

She hadn't seen the cuffs since that first morning when he'd given her a choice between cooperating and fighting him. Well, she'd made her choice, hadn't she? She didn't know he was on to her, and he wasn't about to lay that on her now, when she was in agony. But the fact remained that she couldn't be trusted. He couldn't leave the estate without restraining her.

Unbelievably, his fingers shook as he snapped the cuff around her wrist. He closed his eyes and fought the lead weight that threatened to crush his chest. His fingers lingered on her slender wrist, over the rapid flutter of her pulse.

He opened his eyes and woodenly snapped the other cuff around the headboard's wrought-iron fili-gree, without looking at her. "It won't be for long, Lizzie." When she said nothing, he added, "It has to be this way."

A wrenching sob burst from her as if she'd been struggling to contain it. As she wept, the fingers of her free hand slipped under the ice bag to press on her forehead. He knew her tears were making the pain worse.

He fought the impulse to gather her in his arms. His hand hovered over her anguished face for a moment before tentatively lowering to smooth her hair back.

"Lizzie..." His voice was a hoarse whisper. "Lizzie, don't..."

Through convulsive sobs she got out, "Caleb, please...please don't do this. I'll stay right here...I *promise...."*

He squeezed his eyes shut. He couldn't bear to hear this proud woman plead, despised himself for flaying her dignity this way.

She asked, "What if...what if I get sick again?"

That thought had occurred to him, but it wasn't why he dragged the keys out of his pocket.

Worse than what he was doing to Lizzie was what he was doing to himself. What he was turning himself into. During all his years in the Special Forces, through his grueling training and more-than-grueling missions, he'd never relinquished his humanity. Or his honor.

Lizzie might not have the same high standards of humanity, or honor, but right now she was in no condition to do any harm. Restraining her would serve a punitive function only. There would be time enough for that later.

Caleb unlocked the cuffs and set them aside. He held her small, soft hand between his big, rough ones and rubbed the wrist as if he could erase the last few moments. A weary sigh escaped him, dredged from the depths of his soul. He wondered which of them was going to be more changed by this bizarre interlude in their lives. It was a question that wouldn't have occurred to him three days ago.

Her chin still quivered slightly. "Thank you," she whispered.

His fingers tightened around hers. He shook his head as his gaze burned into hers, but he couldn't bring forth the words to tell her that her gratitude was misplaced. The nature of their relationship hadn't changed. It couldn't. He had a promise to fulfill, to a dead brother he'd failed more than once. Caleb wouldn't allow himself to fail again.

He gave her hand a little squeeze. "Try to rest," he said quietly. "I'll be back as soon as I can."

Before going to the drugstore, Caleb drove around to where he'd seen the model rocket land. It took him only a few minutes to locate it, payload bay intact, at the edge of the woods near a road. It was a miracle no one had stumbled on it yet; he had no doubt it would have been found in the morning. Pure dumb luck had saved his butt not once, but twice today. Earlier, he'd left the garage to get some tools from the shed, and just happened to see the damn thing arc over the distant treetops. A quick perusal of the attic had told him all he needed to know.

Part of him was filled with grudging admiration. He supposed he could be accused of carelessness, but who would have thought she'd do so much with so little? He'd come within a hairbreadth of being arrested for kidnapping.

And convicted. He knew that legal precedent was on Lizzie's side, no matter what slimeball practices Lugh might have employed.

Caleb could have laughed at the irony. Here he was, one of a handful of the most superbly trained warriors in the world, a top expert in explosives—his specialty in the Delta Force—and what weapon does his little commune cutie use against him? A toy rocket!

And it had almost worked.

The part of him that wasn't awestruck at Lizzie's audacious move was sobered by the desperation that led to it. What did she imagine he was going to do to her? Did she think he planned to keep her prisoner forever? Or exact some horrendous revenge for what she'd done to David?

The way Caleb had terrorized her that first night, he wouldn't blame her if she did. It gave him no pleasure to do that to her. God knew he wasn't in the habit of victimizing defenseless women. He'd approached this as just another mission, one he was determined to see through to the end.

That part, at least, hadn't changed. He still had a job to do, for David, even if he found it increasingly difficult to stay focused. He'd be lying to himself if he didn't admit his brother's version of events had always seemed a little...off, especially Lizzie's horrendous treatment of him. If David hadn't been so devastated—if he hadn't killed himself over her!—Caleb might have suspected he'd embellished the facts.

In the few days he'd known Lizzie, those initial doubts about David's story had returned with a vengeance. Could this be the woman his brother had spoken of so scathingly? The woman who'd belittled him, savaged his pride?

Somehow Caleb had a hard time imagining it.

He sat in the Land Rover reading and rereading her message—her appeal for help—before shoving it into the pocket of his black leather jacket.

No. It gave him no pleasure to do that to her.

Lizzie had tried on several occasions to reiterate her story about joining the commune undercover to investigate David's suicide. But even if Caleb were inclined to believe her, the evidence couldn't be denied: she'd given them all her money and let them tattoo her! Those acts bespoke genuine commitment.

Dutiful deprogrammer that he was, he'd attempted to discuss the dangers of Avalon with her, but soon realized the futility of that approach when she pretended to agree with everything he said. Eventually he'd realized she'd have to come around on her own.

He only hoped it wouldn't take too long. Things weren't going exactly the way he'd envisioned. He found he no longer had the stomach for the rough stuff.

And the rough stuff was precisely what he'd promised her if she pulled this kind of stunt.

Mulling over that quandary, he turned the key in the ignition and drove as fast as he dared to the drugstore. By the time he arrived back home, night had descended and a full moon had risen.

When he crept into Lizzie's dark bedroom, she was once more curled up with her back to him. She flinched at the touch of his fingertips on her shoulder. Her voice was frighteningly weak and shaky.

"It's worse...so bad, Caleb." She moaned pitifully, sounding close to tears. "I can't stand it."

Her misery tore at his guts. *Oh, Lizzie...I never meant for this to happen.* He shook out one of the painkillers—a mixture of ergotamine and caffeine. Dr. O'Neal had warned him it would take a while to kick in, and not to expect total relief, since the attack was advanced. He'd also gotten her to prescribe the other medications in Lizzie's pharmaceutical arsenal, to keep this from happening again.

Caleb rolled her over onto her back, wincing when she cried out in pain. Sweat had soaked her clothes, though the room was cool. He raised her and pressed the pill between her lips, following this with a sip of water.

He left her long enough to get the hot water flowing in the tub, then returned and gently eased her out of bed. She was unsteady on her feet, and he put his arm around her and grabbed the fresh ice bag he'd brought up.

"Where are we going?" she asked.

"Dr. O'Neal said a shallow hot bath might help, along with the ice—something about drawing the blood flow from your head."

The full moon shone through the bathroom skylight, providing just enough illumination. But even that was too much for Lizzie, who kept her head down and her eyes covered. She appeared ready to topple without the support of his arm. He turned off the water and started unbuttoning her shirt.

For a few blessed seconds she seemed oblivious to what he was doing, then she jerked as if burned and grabbed his wrists in a futile attempt to stop him. By that time he was nearly at the last button.

"Caleb!" She tried to scowl at him with one eye. If she weren't in so much pain, he would have laughed. "I can do this myself. Go away."

He pulled the damp shirt off her shoulders and down her arms, his movements quick and economical. "Sweetheart, you can't even stand up by yourself. You can't open your eyes. If I leave you alone in here, you'll drown."

The shirt sailed into the hamper. She crossed both arms over her lacy bra while simultaneously snatching at the jeans he was hauling down her legs. She didn't have enough hands.

While he removed her socks, she whined, "I really want privacy, Caleb. If you're worried, just...stand outside the door or something."

He moved behind her to unhook her bra and slide it down her shoulders. He said, "I don't know what you're squawking about. It's pitch-dark in here."

That whopper made her go still long enough for him to free the bra from her grasping fingers and toss it into the hamper.

"You're lying," she accused, her eyes cracking open before squeezing shut. "It's plenty bright."

"It only seems that way 'cause you're sensitive to light right now. I swear to God, I can't see a blessed thing." He pulled her panties down. "I'm going by feel here."

By the time he stepped in front of her, she'd built up a full head of steam, her hands once more clamped over her eyes. *"How can you stand there and tell me these awful lies?"*

"I'm a stinker, Lizzie. I thought you knew that."

Caleb lowered his gaze and stared in helpless awe. Sweet Jesus. She stood naked under the skylight, her breasts and womanly curves dusted with silver, the velvet shadows sweetly mysterious. He'd known since the first night that Lizzie had a beautiful body. Frisking her had been a hands-on lesson, so to speak. But never could he have imagined...

A body like this shouldn't be clothed in worn-out jeans and ratty flannel shirts. If he'd been David, he'd have dressed her in satin and lace...like that yellow silk thing he'd made her change into the first night. When he'd seen her in that, Caleb had nearly choked.

He clenched his fists, sickened at the jealousy that swelled within him when he thought of his brother's hands on her, slipping that sexy nightgown off her shoulders. She'd belonged to David. And she'd destroyed him. He must never forget that.

Dragging his eyes back to her face, he said, "Get in the tub."

"I hate you."

"Seems to me we've covered this ground. Get in the tub, Lizzie."

"Where is it?"

"Right here." He guided her to the edge and helped

her grope her way into it. She slowly sat down, and Caleb folded a towel to tuck behind her head. "Lean back," he said, and placed the ice bag on her forehead. "Keep your hands in the water. That's supposed to help."

"It's hot."

He sat on the edge of the tub. "Too hot?"

"No."

"Then shut up and relax."

He kept her in the bath for more than an hour, letting in more hot water from time to time. It seemed to take forever, but gradually he saw the tension in her body slacken as the pain began to recede.

He rose and stretched out the kinks in his back and stood staring out the skylight at the fat moon overhead. Her voice startled him.

"Is it a full moon?"

Amazingly, her eyes were open and she blinked at the skylight for a few moments. He could tell the light still bothered her.

"As full as it's going to get," he said.

Her head lolled to the side and she yawned. "Full moon..." With a smirk she said, "Wonder what Lugh will do without me to keep him busy tonight."

Caleb sucked in a sharp breath, feeling the pulse throb in his temple. He glanced at the skylight. "Does your revered leader get especially horny when the moon's full?" he asked tightly. But then, she wouldn't know, having arrived at Avalon since the last full moon.

She stretched languidly and slid down in the tub a

little, holding on to the ice pack. "Avalon is a nature-based commune. They're really into the 'rhythms of the earth.' Life revolves around the seasons and the lunar calendar." She wore an unreadable little smile. "Their revered leader's particularly fond of the full moon."

She sounded downright impertinent. Maybe Caleb was getting through to her at last. "Are you ready to come out?" he asked. She yawned again. "You're ready."

He grabbed a thick bath sheet and helped her rise. While she dried off, he said, "It still hurts, doesn't it?"

She nodded. "It's a lot better, though. More like your garden-variety splitting headache."

She wrapped the bath sheet around her and they returned to the dusky bedroom, where he opened a drawer and groped around for a nightgown. He might have missed the exquisitely delicate fabric if his callused fingers hadn't snagged it. He smiled to himself when he saw what he held, having spent a good deal of time examining this particular garment days earlier when he'd searched her storage boxes. It was a sleeveless, pale peach number with lacy netting panels on the front and back in lieu of straps. He slipped it over Lizzie's head and watched it float down her body with a sensual whisper. The bias-cut silk stretched in all the right places. It was almost better than seeing her naked.

Nah...

He observed, "For someone who dresses as frumpy

as you do during the day, you've got one hell of a collection of naughty nighties."

"Is that a compliment or an insult?"

"Why? You keeping track?" He turned down the covers of her bed, flipped her pillow and fluffed it.

She shrugged. "A girl's gotta have a hobby."

"What's the score so far?"

"You really want to know?"

Her words were bantering, nonchalant, but he noticed she didn't meet his eyes. Would it kill him? He said, "Consider it a compliment, Lizzie."

She glanced at him quickly, clearly expecting to see his customary sneer. Not the appreciative smile that he didn't try to suppress. Just as quickly she turned away and climbed into bed, facing the wall. She pulled the covers up.

A minute later his weight made the mattress dip, and she looked over her shoulder. And whipped upright when she saw him sitting there in his briefs, casually pulling off his socks. Her eyes were round, her jaw slack.

"Lie down, Lizzie."

"You can't...you're not—"

"Relax." He slid under the covers and hauled her down with him, to lie spoon fashion with her back to his front. "I told you that's not what I'm after, remember?"

Of course, that was before he'd seen her clad in nothing but moon frost. Still, he had no intention of acting on the primal needs she aroused—in part because he had no taste for predatory females, but mostly because this particular predatory female was at his mercy. He grimaced. His damnable honor and all that.

She said, "I don't want you here, Caleb."

He felt her trying to squirm away from him, but there wasn't a hell of a lot of room to squirm on this dinky double bed, now that she was sharing it with him. Of course, he was accustomed to stretching out diagonally on his king-size mattress.

He slid his palm over her waist to hold her still. The thin silk left nothing to his imagination. He felt her heat, her delicate ribs, the tantalizing indentation of her belly button. Deciding not to push his luck, he moved his hand up to her smooth shoulder. Safer territory.

"I'm staying, Lizzie. You might need something in the middle of the night." *Like liquid propellant or a couple of solid rocket boosters.*

She sighed, whether in resignation or appreciation, he couldn't tell. Minutes passed and he began to think she'd gone to sleep; hoped so, for her sake. Her body heat warmed his front, and he tried to ignore the sweet pressure of her round, silk-clad bottom so close to his...

Damn. *Stop thinking about rockets!*

His mouth brushed her hair, a fall of fragrant gossamer. He dipped his head ever so slightly and parted his lips, to increase the teasing contact.

"Caleb..."

"Hmm?"

He felt her fingers slide over his hand on her shoulder. Her voice was small and whispery, a voice for sharing secrets in the dark. "No one ever took care of me before."

He frowned. *No one?*

She half turned her head, as if sensing his confusion. "Not since...you know...I was a child."

Caleb's frown deepened. What about David? Where had his brother been while the woman he loved suffered these killer migraines alone?

As if she were disclosing something shameful, she said, "I get scared. Sometimes when the pain comes, it's so bad I think crazy things. Like I wish I could just die so it would stop." He felt her shudder. "But I wasn't scared tonight, Caleb. Even when it got real bad, I knew you were coming back and you'd have my medicine and you'd—" she squeezed his hand "—take care of me. And you did."

She turned a little more and looked into his eyes, her own wide and bottomless in the semidark. "Thank you."

Her heartbreaking candor staggered him. What was wrong with this woman? She should curse him for being the cause of her misery, not thank him for the one morsel of human decency he'd shown her.

For the first time he wondered what kind of life Lizzie had had.

She leaned toward him and kissed him on the cheek, a quick, chaste kiss of gratitude. He lay perfectly still, staring at her, absorbing the startling sensation of her warm, soft lips pressed to his skin.

Then she turned back around and settled against him. "Good night, Rambo."

4

ELIZABETH HAD WONDERED what Caleb would do with her when he had to leave the estate—or Fort Trent, as she thought of it—where they'd been sequestered together for more than a week now. Well, she need wonder no more.

"Where do you want to wait for me, Lizzie?"

He towered over her in the big country kitchen. She felt insignificant and downright asinine in his mother's frilly little apron and oven mitts. Two French baguettes had just come out of the oven—long, thin, crusty loaves to sop up the gravy of their beef stew tonight. Thank goodness she loved to cook. There wasn't much else to do at Fort Trent besides cook and read and scheme and pray.

For rescue. She hadn't given up hope that her message in the rocket would be found. It must have landed in a heavily wooded area. Maybe it *had* gotten caught on a high limb and would drop before long. Or get washed up on a lakeshore. She thought of little else.

Her eyes went to the handcuffs dangling from Caleb's fingers, and her stomach turned over. She'd foolishly allowed herself to believe she'd seen the last of them, after he'd relented the night she was so sick. After all, hadn't she been convincing as the obedient, enlightened deprogrammee? And hadn't they gotten along passably well? An outsider peeking into their "home life" would actually believe the domestic tranquillity was genuine. Caleb even said nice things about her cooking!

The two of them had gotten into the habit of jogging together each morning before breakfast. That was the most serene part of the day, when they did their stretching exercises out by the back porch and ran side by side around the estate near the tree line. Serene because it was a strictly physical activity they shared without conversation, without her having to pretend she was something she wasn't. In those charmed moments she could almost believe she was a guest, not a prisoner.

And all the while she bided her time, waiting for all hell to break loose when her rescuers arrived.

She raised her eyes from the cuffs to his face, willing her expression to remain neutral, though she could feel a cold sweat popping out. She hoped she didn't look as pale as she felt. She hated those damn things, the sensation of helpless immobility.

Caleb's gaze slid to the window. "I have to reprovision. We're low on rations."

"So I've noticed." He had milk, eggs, bread and other staples delivered to the front gate twice a week, but they were low on a lot of other things. She pasted on what she hoped would pass for a benign expression. This wasn't the time to blow her image.

She needn't have bothered; he didn't even look at

her. Everything else in the kitchen seemed to hold more interest. "Yeah. Well." He indicated the cuffs. "Where?"

"Um...how long will you be gone?"

He dragged a hand through his thick, light brown hair. "A couple of hours. A little less if the store's not too crowded."

Two hours! She nearly groaned. "How about the sunroom, then?"

He shrugged. "Fine with me."

She shucked the apron and mitts and followed him to the sunroom, where late morning sunshine streamed through the huge, plant-bedecked bay window with its eastern exposure. He steered her to the brass daybed, made up as a sofa with bolsters and a slipcover. Compliantly she sat at the end and offered her left wrist.

As he bent over her to fasten the cuffs, Elizabeth tried to ignore his warmth and the distinctive masculine scent that drifted over her. His face hovered inches from hers, his gray eyes studiously glued to his task. This man had seen her stark naked. That realization only made her feel more helpless and vulnerable.

At the crew neck of his sweater she saw a silver chain, one she'd noticed before. What hung from it? She stared at the mysterious scar on his temple and wondered for the hundredth time how he came by it. His gray sweater sleeves were pushed up and she eyed the jagged pink scar that snaked up his muscular, hair-dusted forearm.

Her mind conjured an image of the armed commando in the field, the man in the snapshot David had carried in his wallet. She thought of Caleb wounded and bleeding in some remote, war-torn corner of the globe; surprisingly, the thought brought no pleasure.

This was the closest they'd been—the closest they'd allowed themselves to be—since the morning after her migraine, when she'd woken in the hot curl of his big body....

Caleb had still been asleep, his massive chest expanding against her back in an even, unhurried cadence. His warm breath stirred her hair and teased her neck. He sighed and tightened his arm over her waist, drawing her closer till she felt an insistent hard ridge against her bottom.

She bit her lip and went still as stone, horrified he'd wake up in that instant. His broad palm pressed on her belly as he angled his hips, sliding his knee over her legs as if to hold her to him. Nothing lay between their bodies but his briefs and a wisp of silk. Slowly, lazily, he flexed into her, throbbed against her, and Elizabeth bit her lip harder, her eyes round with wonder. He felt...enormous. *Is that the way it works?* she asked herself. *Are really big men really big...all over?*

She swallowed hard as his hand crept up her rib cage with agonizing slowness, and she couldn't help but wonder, *Is he dreaming about me?* Through her flimsy nightgown she felt the firm, coarse texture of his hand as it inched upward...marking her.

His thumb grazed the underside of her breast and she stopped breathing. Her eyes drifted shut and she tried to tell herself she didn't want his hand to continue its upward journey. Her nipples pulled into tight knots that scraped the silk when she finally took a ragged breath. She shivered, anticipating how hot his hand would feel there, how his touch would burn her. His fingers started to move—

And stopped abruptly. She felt his body go rigid, felt his heartbeat hammer her back for a few seconds before he rolled away and sat up. She shivered harder at the loss of his heat, of the potent vitality that both terrified and enthralled her. She didn't try to feign sleep, knowing her agitation had to be all too obvious. She'd heard a low, muttered oath...felt an icy emptiness as the door closed behind him.

Now, after days of walking on eggshells and trying not to brush up against him, she could only wonder if he was as edgy as she was. He straightened and stepped away as soon as she was shackled to one of the brass spindles.

He asked, "You need anything before I leave?"

"How about something to read? Anything but *Soldier of Fortune*."

That actually produced a smile, albeit a crooked one. He left and returned a few minutes later with a foot-high stack of *Vogue* magazines. Before she could comment, he leveled a quelling stare and said, "My mother."

"Uh-huh."

And then he was gone, leaving her to flip through three years worth of fashions for the well-heeled recluse. The minutes dragged, and the worst part was that Elizabeth didn't even know how much time had passed—she'd removed her watch before starting to bake. She could only guess at the hour as the shadows shortened and the sun rose high. It was definitely past the time Caleb had promised to be back. She liked *Vogue,* but she didn't like it *that* much.

When her stomach whined and she could no longer ignore her hunger, she realized lunchtime had come and gone. She thought of those fragrant baguettes sitting on the kitchen counter. Her throat was gummy with thirst and she fantasized about dragging the daybed by her shackled wrist to get to that frosty bottle of cola in the fridge.

As midday slid into afternoon, the room **became** a landscape of soft shadows in the diffuse light. A nagging disquiet accompanied the creeping chill. She dumped the magazines on the floor and tossed the bolsters after them, then crawled under the thin, fitted slipcover and curled up, trembling, cursing the immobility that kept her from warming up. There were no sheets, and she was only marginally warmer than before. The bound hand was ice-cold and painfully cramped. But through her discomfort, one question dominated her thoughts.

Could something have happened to Caleb?

She scolded herself. The guy was invulnerable. A tank. What could happen to the commando?

A car accident.

She chewed her lip. Well, that would be good, wouldn't it? An accident could solve all her problems. If he'd been taken to a hospital, someone would try to call the estate, and since they wouldn't get through, they might send someone out....

Okay, maybe not. Well, if he was conscious, wouldn't Caleb alert them that she was here?

If he was conscious. If he was alive. She swallowed hard. She didn't like those ifs. Those ifs made her pulse skitter and her palms sweat. And it wasn't her own predicament she was thinking of.

When it came right down to it, he'd never actually hurt her. Somehow, she doubted he ever would. And she'd never forget how he'd nursed her through her migraine....

A warm hand on her shoulder and a gentle voice in her ear jolted Elizabeth out of a fitful doze. She cried out and jerked her hand against the steel cuff, as pain shot up her arm.

"Lizzie, it's okay, it's me...."

She blinked at Caleb squatting next to the daybed, hurriedly unlocking the handcuffs. She licked her dry mouth and rubbed her face. "What time is it?"

He sighed disgustedly, with a little shake of his head. "Three forty-five." He started to say something—*I'm sorry*?—then stopped himself and simply explained, "The Land Rover broke down. Popped a fan belt. I had to get it towed, and then wait around...." He held her fingers between his palms. "God, your hands are like ice." He started absently rubbing her fingers. It felt like heaven.

"Don't stop," she mumbled.

He hesitated, as if only then realizing what he'd been doing. Then he started again, more carefully, systematically. His hands were as powerful as the rest of him, but he seemed to know just how much pressure to exert as he massaged and kneaded her hands from the wrist to the fingertips.

"Better?" he asked at last. She nodded. "You must be starving."

She nodded again. "And thirsty. And I wish I hadn't had three cups of coffee this morning. But mainly...I was just so scared."

He squeezed her hand. "I know, Lizzie. I really thought I'd be back by—"

"I thought something happened to you."

He frowned. "To me?"

She sat up shakily, tossing off the slipcover and rubbing her arms. "Like an accident." She looked him in the eye, unable to disguise the fear that had consumed her for the last couple of hours. "I thought you were hurt, Caleb. Lying in a...in a hospital somewhere. Or worse."

He studied her face, his expression intense, probing. He released her hand. "You thought you'd die chained to this damn bed," he said brusquely.

She averted her eyes so he wouldn't see the unshed tears that stung them. She shook her head in response, because she couldn't speak.

His weary exhalation broke the silence. He stood and laid a gentle hand on her shoulder...and then she understood. He knew she'd been worried for him, not herself, but he couldn't admit it. To her or perhaps even to himself. Because feelings like that weren't part of his well-orchestrated mission.

He patted her shoulder. "I'll put away the groceries. You rest."

"Rest?" She laughed while sniffing back tears. "You've got to be kidding."

After a detour to the bathroom, she went to the kitchen, guzzled that cold cola and helped him unload bags of groceries from the Land Rover. She began unpacking them, tearing open packages and filling her empty belly in the process. She reached into a bag and pulled out a small can. Grinning, she brandished it in Caleb's face.

"Friskies Buffet?" If she didn't know better, she'd swear that was a hint of pink under Rambo's three-o'clock shadow. She peered into the sack. "Good Lord, Caleb, how many did you buy?"

"It's cheaper than tuna," he snapped. "Natasha won't know the difference."

"Natasha?"

Caught! his expression said. "Give me those!" He grabbed the bag, stalked to a high cabinet and started stowing the cans.

Elizabeth was right behind him. "I've gotta know how you came up with 'Natasha.'"

His broad shoulders slumped in defeat. "Boris and Natasha. You know. Maybe you're too young to remember." He slathered on a thick Russian accent. "Get moose and squirrel."

"Ah. So you named your new pet for a sullen cartoon spy-slash-vamp."

"Natasha was no vamp. Don't be misled by that slinky black dress."

"Black. I get it. A black cat."

"A skinny black cat with a snotty disposition."

"Okay, I'll buy it. What are you going to name the kittens? Rocky and Bullwinkle?"

"That animal is not mine!" He plunked the last can in the cabinet and slammed the door. "The damn thing's never coming in the house."

Elizabeth shook her head, with a little smile. Men. The spike-chomping commando didn't stand a chance.

He said, "There's a case of soda still in the car," and disappeared through the doorway.

Alone in the kitchen, Elizabeth noticed Caleb's black leather jacket hanging on a peg. Her survival instincts kicked in as she recognized this rare opportunity. She didn't think he'd actually be careless enough to leave a key or weapon where she could get to it, but how would she know unless...

One eye on the door, she clawed through the pockets. Loose change, the receipt for the fan belt, a pack of tissues... She smiled, remembering her astonishment when he'd helped her blow her nose that first night while she stood helplessly bound and gagged. At that point her abductor had been a savage, faceless killer. Over the past week he'd metamorphosed into a complex man whose motivations she could almost sympathize with. Almost.

She dug in the last pocket and came up with a crumpled piece of paper. Too big for a cash-register receipt. She smoothed it out, saw what it was and felt an iron ball slam into her chest.

"No..." she groaned, feeling the room tilt sickeningly as she scanned the note she'd tucked into the rocket five days ago. Her one hope for salvation. She blinked as her vision dimmed, and groped blindly to steady herself.

A pair of strong hands seized her forearms, spun her around and pulled her against a warm, firm, woolly expanse that could only be Caleb's sweater-clad chest. She felt his hands on her back and her head, holding her secure.

"Sit down and put your head between your knees," he ordered.

Gulping air, her heart bucking violently, she wrenched away from him. Unadulterated hatred helped her eyes and her mind snap into sharp focus, and she threw the wadded-up note at him. He caught it and glanced at it briefly, then tossed it across the room into the garbage. His face was impassive.

"You bastard," she hissed. "You let me think..." Elizabeth swallowed convulsively, her rage threatening to choke her. She knew how wild-eyed and out of control she must appear, but she didn't give a damn. "You let me hope...and all the time..." She gestured helplessly, dry-eyed, too shattered for tears.

A hint of regret marred his gruff tone. "You shouldn't have tried it, Lizzie."

"How could you let me keep waiting...praying? Day after day...when you *knew* it was hopeless? You made a fool out of me." This was worse than anything else he'd done. "Why? *Why*, Caleb? In the name of

God, why didn't you *tell* me you found the damn note?"

His expression was fiercer than she'd ever seen it. "Why the hell do you *think* I didn't tell you? We both know what I promised if you tried to escape. Is that what you *want?*" he shouted. "That kind of brutality?"

He slammed a fist into a cabinet, rattling the contents. "I should've played it that way from the start. The hell with this *civilized*, hands-off approach." He took a menacing step closer. "How about it, Lizzie? A traditional, brutal deprogramming. Just you and me. Twenty-four hours—two days, tops—and we're done with it. Done with each other. For good."

That last part struck her like a slap, when the prospect should have thrilled her. *Done with each other.*

He said, "And let me assure you, sweetheart, once I deprogram you, you'll stay deprogrammed. It's not an experience you'll want to repeat."

Elizabeth didn't think, she reacted. The instant he reached for her, she picked up a kitchen chair and swung it at him. As he dodged it, she let momentum carry the chair in a full arc to sweep several full grocery bags from the table onto the floor. It felt damn good, until Caleb seized her from behind and twisted the chair out of her grasp.

"That's enough!" he rasped.

She fought him desperately, fury infusing her with a strength she'd never known. Nevertheless, he subdued her easily, wrapping his powerful arms around her like a human straitjacket.

She felt the warm buzz of his taunting voice on her scalp. "You really gave a flawless performance, you know that? Acting so meek and spineless for days on end. There were a couple of times—like today—when even *I* thought you should scratch my eyes out. If I hadn't discovered your little foray into rocket science, I might've actually bought it."

Panting, sweating, with her hair draping her eyes, she squirmed harder, and he tightened his arms till she could barely breathe. "Show's over, I guess," he observed. "Sort of refreshing to find out the real Lizzie has some backbone."

He spun her around, and she lashed out with a savage kick to his shin as her nails arced toward his eyes. He caught her wrist just in time, grunting, "Didn't mean to give you ideas," as he hoisted her over his shoulder. "I know a good place for you to cool down."

Déjà vu. Only this time her hands were free. He wanted backbone? As he stalked into the pantry, she yanked up his gray sweater and sank her teeth into the solid muscle of his lower back, wishing there were a soft, flabby spot somewhere so she could get a better grip. He bellowed and skidded to a stop, jiggling her roughly in a futile attempt to dislodge her incisors.

"Let go!" he demanded.

Her response was to chomp harder, tenacious as a lamprey. He cursed and jabbed his fingertips into the sensitive flesh under her ribs, forcing her jaws to unlock with a gasp. He threw her off him forcefully and she staggered against a freestanding, wooden shelving unit. Her eyes flicked to the cartons and canisters piled on it.

"Don't even think about—" he started to say, and leaped away as the entire shelving unit crashed down, spewing cereal, rice, sugar and flour over the floor.

She said, "The new me. What do you think?"

He filled the doorway, breathing hard, surveying the damage. His voice was dangerously low and controlled. "You're going to clean up every goddamn crumb, Lizzie. And when you're done, you're gonna start on the kitchen."

She hurled the vilest obscenity she could think of.

He snorted. "If you ask me nicely, I'll teach you how to swear." He stepped out and slammed the door. She heard the lock snick.

Immediately Elizabeth dragged the step stool under the one high, tiny window and forced it open. She boosted herself up to the sill and, grasping the window frame, hooked a leg up. She started wriggling through, feetfirst, and nearly got stuck halfway. Only the thought of Caleb finding her like this gave her the incentive to finally squeeze through. It was a long drop to the ground. The instant her toes made contact, she was off, sprinting across the lawn.

It was cold and she didn't have her jacket, but the glowing ball of hatred in her gut warmed her from the inside out. At that moment nothing mattered except putting as much distance as possible between herself and her jailer.

5

WHEN WAS HE GOING to stop underestimating this woman? Wasn't that the fundamental rule of warfare—never underestimate your enemy?

Caleb stood at the entrance to the pantry, staring at the hellish mess on the floor and the open window high in the back wall. Hell, she hadn't done anything he wouldn't have. Not that he'd have had a prayer of fitting through that little window. No, he'd have gone after the door lock.

He left the house and strolled toward the tree line, wondering whether to wait her out or track her down in the woods. She must be freezing. Dusk was approaching and she'd been outside without a jacket for nearly an hour, assuming she'd escaped the instant he'd locked the door—a pretty good bet. He smiled grimly. When he caught up to her, she'd probably pull a tree down on his head.

He found himself at the edge of the woods, peering through the bare limbs, alert for any sign of movement. Her voice overhead made him jump.

"Too bad I don't have one of those rocks you seem so worried about...." She was leaning casually in the window of his old tree house twelve feet up, a moth-eaten blanket draped serape-style over her shoulders.

She disappeared from the window and reemerged at the doorway, where she sat with her feet dangling over the rope ladder. "If I did, I could've clobbered you with it, snatched your keys and let the cops wake you up."

He crossed his arms over his chest and treated her to his most devastating smirk. "Yeah, too bad."

She sighed. "All I have is this big old brick someone left on the roof." She opened the blanket to display her newfound weapon.

Caleb's smile gradually faded as he blinked at the heavy, mortar-encrusted brick on her lap, the same brick he'd placed on the roof of the tree house twenty years ago to hold down the ill-fitting trapdoor leading to the rooftop "observation deck."

Damn. He'd underestimated her again!

With the wisdom of hindsight he analyzed his critical error. Back before he'd kidnapped her, when he'd "Lizzie-proofed" the house and grounds, he'd labored under dangerously inaccurate assumptions. He'd seen her as a one-dimensional femme fatale, a shallow heartbreaker whose talents extended only to snaring and destroying unsuspecting men. The intelligence, pride and determination he'd witnessed the last week had never entered into the equation.

Maybe he should go over the place one more time.

Meanwhile, he just had to know...

"Why didn't you do it, Lizzie? Why didn't you knock me out with that brick and escape? It would've worked."

She simply stared down at him with those enormous, solemn brown eyes. Finally she said quietly, "Not my style."

What would be Lizzie's "style"? The hairs on his nape sprang to attention. She'd once tweaked him with a veiled reference to poisonous plants. At the time, he'd laughed it off as bluster. Was he underestimating her yet again?

Perhaps, but hadn't she confessed her fears for his safety when he was so late today? As he'd watched her eyes glaze with tears, there'd been no doubt in his mind her distress was genuine. Somehow he couldn't imagine Lizzie doing him violence—herbal or otherwise. No matter how far he pushed her.

He said, "Come into the house, Lizzie."

"I don't think so."

He sighed. "Are you going to make me come up there after you?"

"Are you going to make me find out what I can do with this brick?" she asked pleasantly, stroking the thing like a pet.

He hesitated. Come to think of it, perhaps he *had* pushed her too far. "You've gotta be cold."

She indicated the blanket.

He said, "That thing's been up there for years. It's probably infested." That should do the trick.

She snuggled deeper into the blanket. "Well then, we'll all keep each other warm." Delicately she sniffed the mangy wool. "If they don't mind the smell, I don't."

He should have known. If she wasn't scared of *him*, she sure as hell wasn't going to swoon from a few bugs. He was tempted to leave her out here—all night if need be—but something told him there was a fundamental issue he was neglecting, something that went deeper than simple muleheadedness.

What had he learned about Lizzie during their brief time together? What was keeping her from capitulating, from coming to her senses? What did she need that she wasn't getting?

The same thing you need, an unwelcome inner voice answered. *The same thing everyone needs.*

Respect.

It went against classic deprogramming methods, with their emphasis on belittling and humiliating the subject, but hey, hadn't he always been a maverick?

And face it. Hadn't she earned his respect? At least a little?

He studied the ground at his feet for a few moments, then looked up and said carefully, "You've thrown me for a loop, Lizzie. I've gotta admit, you're not at all what I expected."

"What David led you to expect."

"Well...yeah."

"I knew David for six years. We were very good friends. But that's all it was, Caleb. Friendship."

He started to silence her, still determined to keep her from weaving her tapestry of lies. But a glimpse of the intensity in those lovely eyes pulled him up short. He said, "The relationship my brother described went way beyond 'friendship.'"

She sighed. "I knew he felt...well, more than that for me, at first, but I made it clear that's all it could be and he seemed to accept it. We used to get together a lot, sometimes just the two of us, sometimes with this group of people we're tight with. I could talk to David about anything. And he could talk to me. We were like...best buddies. I don't know how else to put it. He dated a few women, but was never really serious about anyone.

"I thought this...crush on me was a thing of the past. Just some fleeting infatuation he'd gotten over long ago. Turned out he never got over it, just spent six years disguising it." Her expression was bleak. "Last spring he was dating this wonderful woman. Isabelle. She was in love with him, wanted a commitment. I couldn't believe it when he dumped her. I told him he was nuts to let her go, that he'd never find a better woman and should give the relationship a chance."

Her wry smile spoke volumes. "It...wasn't what he wanted to hear. Not from me. That's when it all came out. He'd been biding his time for six years, hoping I'd come around and return his feelings. It wasn't the simple crush I'd once thought, it was more like...an obsession."

She looked him in the eye. "I tried to let him down easy, Caleb. I was as gentle as I knew how to be."

"I'm not buying it, Lizzie. It started out as friendship, what you two had, but it turned into something more, something hot and heavy. You two talked about marriage."

"Never!"

"You waited till he was totally dependent on you

emotionally, at his most vulnerable. Then you yanked the rug out from under him. Rejected him in the most brutal way—"

"No...no!" She was shaking her head.

"Demeaned him. Ridiculed his pathetic devotion to you. Taunted him with your infidelities—"

"Stop! Caleb, stop it! Do you really think I'm capable of something like that?" Her eyes burned with tears of indignation. Hot color spotted her cheeks.

Hadn't he asked himself that very question, more than once? *Could Lizzie have done those things?*

He held her stare, even when he saw her lips tremble, even when he realized with a sick jolt what had wounded her: not his brother's accusations, but Caleb's own unquestioning acceptance of them. His lack of faith in her.

He sucked in a steadying breath, propped up his resolve by sheer strength of will, when it threatened to buckle. Forced himself to look into her stricken eyes when instinct commanded him to turn away from the raw pain he saw there.

"It was all some kind of sick game to you, wasn't it, Lizzie? To see how far you could push my brother before he cracked. Was it diverting, at least? Were the results as dramatic as you'd hoped? Must be flattering as hell having someone kill himself over you. Something to brag about at the beauty parlor."

He had to give her credit—she took it without flinching, as if she was simply waiting for him to wind down, to get it out of his system. Her flat expression bespoke disappointment in him.

He looked away first. Self-doubt bubbled up like acid. He could taste it.

After an eternity she said, "Caleb, you must know your brother was emotionally immature. Manipulative, even."

"David may have been a little...insecure, but he wasn't the basket case you're making out."

"I suspect you don't know these things about him because you weren't around much."

If she'd walloped him with that brick, she couldn't have struck a more hurtful blow. Caleb was all too aware off how little he'd been around for the fatherless boy who looked up to him. David had grown up smothered by their weak, introverted mother. Caleb was the nearest thing the kid had had to a stable male role model, but he'd gone off to West Point when David was ten, and never saw much of him after that.

If David had turned out to be less than the man he should have been, wasn't Caleb at least partly to blame? It was a question that had tormented him in the months since his little brother had put a noose around his neck.

Had Caleb been too quick to attribute David's self-destructive impulses to Lizzie's brutal rejection? Too eager to buy in to the whole sordid story? Certainly it was less harrowing to blame some nameless, faceless heartbreaker than to confront his own failings as a brother and a role model.

Perhaps he should have allowed Lizzie to remain nameless and faceless. How much easier to condemn her before he knew her as a three-dimensional woman, a resourceful, sable-eyed temptress with an interest in French cooking and rocket science.

When Caleb remained silent, Lizzie said, "David revered you, you know."

"I know," he said hoarsely.

"And he had to know how much you'd despise the Avalon Collective. Has it occurred to you that he might have made all this up as an excuse for his actions?"

"What are you saying?"

She leaned forward, crossing her arms on the brick. "By blaming me, by telling you *I'm* the reason he joined Avalon, he sidestepped the truth."

"Which is...?"

"That he joined Avalon of his own free will," she said firmly. "A conscious decision. He wasn't the first to opt for the communal life-style, and he won't be the last. He couldn't admit that to you, Caleb. I don't think he could face your disapproval."

His hands clenched. "You're saying David took the coward's way out."

She couldn't have offered a lower insult to his brother's memory. Why had he let her start talking? She'd had more than a week to work on her story.

He said, "I get the feeling you're trying to convince yourself as much as me. Own up to it, Lizzie. You're responsible for what happened to David."

That much was still true, though he conceded that the issue was far more complex than he'd originally thought.

She sighed. "If I'm responsible for any of this—"

she studied the brick nestled in her lap, picking at the flecks of mortar "—it's because I wouldn't sleep with him. He made a lot out of that—set me up as some sort of model of feminine purity, I guess. Anyway, it only encouraged his obsession."

"I have a hard time with that one, Lizzie. You expect me to believe you two never—"

"I'm a virgin."

The laughter erupted from him before he could check it. She regarded him with stony patience, looking very small and childlike on her high perch, swaddled in that nasty old blanket. "Lizzie..." He chuckled, pressing a hand to his heart. "God help me, I'm trying to keep an open mind, but you gotta work with me, sweetheart. You're what? Twenty-three? Twenty-four?"

"Twenty-five."

"Even if I believed you've kept it under wraps for a quarter of a century, the fact is, you just spent three weeks at Avalon."

"It's not that kind of place."

"No, but the Exalted Grand High Poobah is that kind of guy. Constantly on the prowl for tender young morsels like yourself. And as I understand it, what Lugh wants, Lugh generally gets. Sweetheart. Come on." Caleb's mocking expression urged her to fess up. "You weren't scouring the john the *whole* time!"

"No, I was looking for clues—"

He raised a palm. "That nonsense again. I'd rather hear about Lugh's proclivities, but since you're not so inclined..." He pointed to the house. "Get your fanny back in there, on the double. That's one hellacious mess you made, and you're going to get to work on it right now."

"No."

He kept one eye on the brick. "Oh yes, Lizzie. You're gonna pick up every damn thing, sweep the floors and scrub them." While part of him insisted he take a hard line, another part of him empathized with her defiant outburst, the culmination of eight days of impotent rage. It wouldn't hurt to let her salvage some dignity. "And I'm going to help you," he added.

She looked at him sharply, as if sensing a trick.

He said, "Call it my thanks for all those times you refrained from scratching my eyes out."

"Even though you deserved it."

"Even though I deserved it."

"Here, catch." She tossed the brick, and he barely jumped away in time. "Something else for your chamber of horrors." She threw off the blanket.

"My what?" He was captivated by the sight of her jeans-clad bottom descending the rope ladder. Halfway down she shot a narrow-eyed look over her shoulder. He quickly bent down to retrieve the brick.

"You know...your chamber of horrors," she said when she reached the ground. "The locked room where you keep all those dangerous objects. Juice glasses. Paperweights. Grapefruit spoons." She shuddered dramatically. "Scary to think of all that destructive potential in the hands of one man."

He steered her toward the house. "You sweep, I'll hold the dustpan."

AN EARSPLITTING CLAP of thunder jolted Elizabeth awake just before dawn. As she lay in bed listening to the pounding rain and the accompanying low rumbles, she resigned herself to the fact that she was up for the day. She rose, pulled on her old pink terry-cloth robe and made her way downstairs to put on a pot of coffee.

In the four days since she'd discovered her SOS note in Caleb's pocket and abandoned all hope of rescue, her interactions with her "host" had become more natural and relaxed. She'd dropped the pretense of submissiveness, while taking care not to provoke him. Unfortunately, he considered any attempt to explain her presence in Avalon highly provoking. Still, he seemed to treat her with a greater regard nowadays, his attitude almost one of respect. She considered it ironic that if they'd met under less outlandish circumstances, the two of them might actually have become friends.

Or something more. She refused to lie to herself and deny the attraction that sizzled between them. His masterful self-assurance, the unwavering strength of his convictions, were as arousing as they were frustrating. She'd never known a man like Caleb, never thought herself particularly drawn to powerful, take-charge men.

But this particular take-charge man had awakened something deep within her—something profound, elemental—and somehow she knew she'd never be the same. When he finally released her and she went back to her old life, this restless hunger would forever be a part of her.

And just as surely, she knew she'd never find the man who could ease this gut-deep ache and make her whole. This, then, would be the bitterest relic of her imprisonment, her captor's ultimate revenge.

As she passed the sunroom, lightning illuminated it through the huge bay window, and she stopped cold.

He was in there, facing the window. His back was to her, his arms crossed over his chest.

Many times she'd imagined the body under the bulky sweaters. Now she was forced to admit she didn't have much of an imagination. Caleb wore only gray sweatpants, which hung low on his hard, trim waist. The rapid lightning flashes sketched a bronze torso more powerful, more *male*, than she could have envisioned.

"You gonna just stand there?" he asked, not turning.

She grimaced. It wasn't fair. If Caleb wanted to, he could sneak up on her in a tomb wearing a suit of armor. She, on the other hand, couldn't even make it past him barefoot during a thunderstorm!

She entered the room and stood next to him before the window. "Some storm," she said.

"Uh-huh."

His voice was strained. Had she violated a private moment? Then again, he *had* asked her in. Sort of. She glanced at his face and was astonished to see the tightness around his mouth and eyes. Beads of sweat glistened over his upper lip. Now that she was close, she could discern the tension in his entire body.

"Something wrong?" she asked, an instant before another thunderclap roared.

Caleb flinched, though she could tell he was trying not to. For long moments her rational mind refused to acknowledge what her senses already had: he was afraid of lightning and thunder.

But that was impossible. The *commando*, afraid of thunderstorms?

A few seconds later the house shook with a deafening thunderclap that simultaneously lit the sky. That one was close! His eyes shut briefly, as if against his will. She saw his throat working.

"Caleb...are you af—" She bit her lip. You couldn't ask Rambo a thing like that.

He looked at her, and she averted her eyes. She heard his harsh exhalation, then, "I've always had this stupid phobia, as long as I can remember."

"But...you're an explosives expert!"

He shrugged. "Not the same thing."

Somehow his ready admission seemed a more manly response than denying the obvious. She said, "Well, a phobia's nothing to be asham—"

His blistering look told her to can the platitudes.

What was he trying to accomplish by standing in front of this huge window, exposing himself to his fears? Of course, she supposed it was preferable to cringing in some dark corner. Her eye was caught by a glint of silver on his chest, above his folded arms. She crossed in front of him to finally discover what hung from that chain.

The tiny pendant was obscured, nestled within the dark, swirling hair of his chest. She glanced up at his face to find him staring at her, his eyes more pewter now than silver, the same color as the sky, with dawn struggling to assert itself. She burrowed her fingertips into the crisp curls and lifted the pendant, startled at the unexpected sense of intimacy that gripped her. She held a tiny silver cross, obviously handcrafted and exquisitely simple.

He said quietly, "It was my mother's."

She nodded. Her fingers curled around the cross, warmed by his skin, and his chest rose and fell against her knuckles. She unfurled her fingers and pressed her palm over the cross, over the powerful, steady beat of his heart. Almost against her will, she dragged her gaze back up to his face, to find those pale, penetrating eyes scrutinizing her, as if to turn her inside out and lay her secrets bare.

As more thunder rumbled, he stiffened and the heartbeat under her palm drummed faster. His arms unfolded and she felt his hands on her elbows, sliding upward. Another clap of thunder and his fingers bit into her terry-clad arms.

Never relinquishing her eyes, he murmured, "Now you know my secret. What's yours? What are you afraid of?" After a moment he cupped her cheek, his expression sad and gentle. Had he read her mind? "Lizzie...you must know I could never hurt you."

Without warning, the sky exploded in a violent barrage of thunderclaps accompanied by pulsating bursts of light. He trembled slightly as he pulled her close and brushed his lips over her temple, nuzzling her. She could barely breathe. Her nerve endings felt almost painfully sensitized. Even the gentle nudging of his nose and his abrasive, unshaven chin sent helpless shivers through her. The now-familiar scent of him was a narcotic, rushing to her head and stealing all reason.

Alarmed by the sound of her own soft, panting breaths, she tried to pull away, but he held her fast, thrusting his long, strong fingers through her hair, tilting her head up. Just before his mouth closed over hers, she looked into his eyes...and felt her pulse skid. Never had she seen a man look so predatory.

His warm lips raked hers with savage insistence. When she stubbornly refused to open her mouth, he slid the rough pad of his thumb over the seam of her lips and between them, with just enough pressure to force them open. His strong, lithe tongue plunged and retreated in a primitive and unmistakable rhythm. A shudder rippled through her, settling as a thumping, clutching hunger between her legs. His deep groan vibrated into her, rocking her to her toes. The storm still raged, but he barely seemed to notice.

"Caleb!" she gasped, wresting her swollen lips from his.

Impatiently he yanked at the cloth tie of her robe and tore it open, revealing her white silk nightgown. His fiery gaze scorched her, from her breasts down to the dark triangle she knew to be just visible under the thin white silk.

He drew his fingertips up the side of her breast, and she moaned. His hot palm cupped the weight and caressed her with unexpected tenderness. His thumb and forefinger met and captured the tight, burning peak, which seemed somehow connected to the empty center of her. She cried out hoarsely, grabbing his wrist in panic as a dizzying rush of damp heat overwhelmed her senses.

He caught her around the waist. "Lizzie..." he whispered, "make love with me. Take me inside you."

"Yes..." Never had she felt more raw, more exposed, more aching, than at that frightening moment when the thread of her resistance snapped and she yielded to her desire.

His head swiveled and his eyes locked on the daybed in the shadows behind them. He tugged her robe off as he led her the short distance and sat with her on the bed. He pressed his lips to hers sweetly, cherishingly, then dropped soft kisses on her face and throat. He turned her around and she felt him lift her hair and kiss her shoulder and the back of her neck.

His fingers slipped around to the front, to the row of tiny, silk-covered buttons at the top of her gown. Her eyes fluttered shut as he eased the first button through the buttonhole—then the next button, and the next, as her heart slammed erratically in anticipation. Slowly he slipped the straps down her arms. And grew still.

Confused, she opened her eyes and glanced over her shoulder...and felt a chill crawl over her scalp. He was staring at the little sun tattoo on her shoulder blade, the same mark his brother had borne at the end of his life. When Caleb raised his eyes to her face, they were hard, searching.

"You were very good, you know," he said quietly, and the chill raced from her scalp down her spine. He touched the tattoo, then drew his hand away as if she were soiled. "Is this how it started with David? Did you play on his weaknesses, his vulnerabilities? Is that how you got close to him?"

His words squeezed her heart. "Caleb, don't..." she pleaded.

"Only you didn't have to wait for a storm with my brother, did you?" He jerked as a peal of thunder reinforced his words. "With his insecurities, he must've been pathetically easy to manipulate."

Elizabeth tried to rise, but he shoved her down onto her back, seizing her wrists in one hand and pinning her body down. He loomed over her, more predatory than ever. The tiny silver cross dangled from his neck, glinting in the dim, lightning-studded dawn.

With a bitter chuckle, he said, "Yeah, you were damn good, sweetheart. I know your history, and even *I* almost fell for it. Of course, you can writhe and moan all you like, but there are some things even the best actress can't fake."

Shock held her immobile as he thrust a hand under her gown and between her legs, his touch swift and impersonal. A mortified sob broke from her when his fingers found her wet and undeniably aroused.

As his eyes widened in astonished comprehension,

she gasped out, "You bastard!" Summoning all her strength, she bucked and twisted, lunging from under him to fall heavily to the floor.

"Lizzie!"

She stumbled to her feet at a run, pulling her straps up, feeling him snatch at the back of her gown as she tore across the room.

"Lizzie, wait!"

She ran down the hall and into the foyer, but caught herself at the bottom of the stairs. No. There was no place in this house where he couldn't get to her, and she couldn't bear to face him in her humiliation. On reflex she dashed through the foyer to the front door and fumbled with the locks, her fingers trembling violently. She heard him calling her from the hallway. The damn door wouldn't open!

With desperate urgency she turned the locks clockwise, counterclockwise. She yanked on the doorknob, sobbing in frustration as she heard his voice in the foyer behind her.

"Lizzie, no!"

She shot a glance over her shoulder to see him charging toward her. Her sweaty fingers worked the locks, tugged on the door, and it opened!

She flung herself out of the house at a dead run. Instantly her hair and gown were plastered to her body by the icy, wind-driven rain. Caleb yelled something that she couldn't make out. She hazarded a glance back to see his dark shape in the doorway, his face turned up as lightning forked overhead.

She tripped over a root and sprawled on the wet

grass, but was up instantly, running toward the tree house. She started up the rope ladder, then stepped down and began tugging at one of the stakes securing the last rung to the ground. Cursing under her breath, she yanked and twisted till the thing finally wiggled loose. She freed the other stake, then started climbing.

The ladder was perilously unstable without its anchoring stakes, and her knuckles slammed against the bark all the way up, till they were raw and bleeding. At last she crawled through the doorway and pulled the ladder up after her.

She scooted over the plywood floor and huddled miserably in a puddle against the back wall, hugging herself. Water cascaded around the edges of the ill-fitting trapdoor in the ceiling, because the brick weighting it had been removed. There wasn't a dry spot in the tree house.

Now that the frenzy of her flight was past, she trembled with cold and shame. She'd been ready to give herself to Caleb.... Never had she felt anything like the closeness they'd shared in those few magic moments, the driving need to be joined with him.

At least she was safe for the time being. He'd never come after her in this thunderstorm—his phobia wouldn't let her. Pulling up the ladder was her extra bit of insurance.

"Lizzie!"

She jumped at the sound of his voice bellowing through the rain and thunder, as her heart tried to squeeze through her throat. She crawled on all fours till she could just see out the open doorway, wishing she'd thought to close it behind her.

He was in the yard!

Here was the warrior, the man in David's snapshot, standing twenty yards away in the lashing downpour, methodically scanning the grounds for signs of his quarry. She crept back a little, keeping out of sight even as she stared at him, mesmerized. He seemed oblivious to the cold rain sluicing down his naked torso, molding his sweatpants to his powerful legs, though he tensed visibly at every thunderclap.

As if sensing her eyes on him, Caleb slowly turned his head and locked gazes with her. Or seemed to—she knew he couldn't see her deep in the shadows, yet she froze with dread all the same. In that instant she empathized with every enemy this formidable man had faced as a commando. How could they stand a chance?

He slowly stalked toward her, his gaze fixed, and she scurried back to the far wall, forcing herself to breathe. Suddenly she realized that the ancient tree she sat in was the tallest one on the estate. She swallowed hard, and yelped at the next thunderclap, all too aware she'd taken refuge in a lightning magnet. Oh well, at least that was one more thing that would keep Caleb away.

When several minutes had passed, she allowed herself to relax. Not even Rambo would stay outside in this hellish storm with no chance of reaching his objective. She smiled at her own quick thinking as her gaze came to rest on the heap of rope and slats lying use-lessly on the floor.

A head popped into view in the doorway and she screamed. Caleb hauled himself up and clambered into the tree house, as Elizabeth rose on wobbly legs. He kicked the rope ladder, hurling it outside to clatter against the tree. She noticed his arms and chest were scraped, his pants torn.

He'd climbed the tree to get to her!

He stood backlit in the tiny room, his head nearly brushing the ceiling as rainwater trickled over him through the loose trapdoor. She couldn't make out his expression at first, and for that she was thankful—his tense stance was revealing enough. But then he moved toward her, and soft light from the window caught his face, chiseling his taut features and making his eyes seem to glow from within.

His hunger was a living thing, radiating from him in waves as his gaze traveled down her body. Her wet gown was transparent and clung to her skin. He closed the distance between them and grabbed two handfuls of silk, pulling the gown up and off her in one swift motion. Her body responded immediately with a renewed surge of throbbing heat.

He pulled off his sweatpants and she glimpsed the awesome and startling proof of his desire in the in-stant before he lifted her by the hips and crushed her to the rough plywood wall. Her legs encircled his waist as he tilted her hips to receive him. She clung to his shoulders, staring up at him, transfixed by his in-tensity.

His eyes never left hers as he pressed the rigid tip into her. She gasped at the burning pressure and reflexively arched away, digging her nails into his shoulders. He stopped immediately, not yet truly penetrating her, his expression one of startled disbelief. He stared at her as if he'd never seen her before, and she knew he felt the constriction that told him he would be her first.

His body quivered with strain; his fierce grimace betrayed the supreme effort he was making not to plunge into her and finish what he'd started. Even as her body and heart clamored for completion, he pulled away and released her.

Trembling, she slid down the wall and watched him turn and stagger to the doorway. He grasped the door frame with both hands and leaned out into the storm, flexing his powerful back, letting the icy needles of rain batter his unappeased body. Lightning flashes illuminated his magnificent form. He shook his head as if to clear it and raised his face to the hammering rain.

Elizabeth crawled unsteadily to where her nightgown lay in a puddle. She struggled to tug the garment over her head, but the wet silk clung to itself and to her, twisting around her nose and mouth. Panicking, half-suffocated, she finally pulled it down and pushed her sodden hair off her face.

And found herself alone.

6

NINE...

Caleb riveted his concentration on the weight-laden barbell resting on his shoulders behind his neck. Standing with knees slightly bent, he slowly pushed the bar straight up till his arms were fully extended, then just as slowly lowered it, counting his repetitions. He'd hoped the exertion of a tough workout in his basement gym would occupy his mind as well as his body, and keep unwelcome thoughts at bay.

No such luck.

Ten...eleven...

Sweat trickled down his bare chest and stung the fresh abrasions he'd earned climbing that tree this morning to get at—

Twelve...

—a virgin.

In his mind's eye he saw Elizabeth as she'd looked at the very moment he began to unthinkingly drive himself into her body. She'd stared straight into his eyes, her own wide with trepidation...longing. Trust.

Thirteen...fourteen...

His body quivered from more than physical strain. When he thought of how close he'd come to savagely taking her virginity against the wall of that damn tree house, he felt sick with self-disgust. Hell, you couldn't come much closer. The effort of holding back had taken more raw grit than he'd known he had.

Thank God he'd found that grit, somewhere deep within himself. In that stunning instant when he'd realized what he was about to do, it had all come crashing in on him like a tidal wave—all the reasons he'd been so careful, for so long, to keep her at arm's length. The most important reason being her helplessness, the fact that she was under his control.

Fifteen.

He eased the barbell over his head and lowered it to the floor for a short break between sets. Flexing his hands in his fingerless weight-lifting gloves, he grabbed a towel from his workout bench and mopped his face and chest. After a minute he hefted the barbell and began his third set. And nearly dropped it on his head when Elizabeth's voice rang out behind him.

"A roomful of heavy, blunt objects. Be still, my heart!"

He carefully lowered the bar to his shoulders and glanced over it to see her standing in the doorway. Despite her droll greeting, she didn't meet his eyes. She held herself with telling stiffness, hands stuffed into the kangaroo pocket of her long, light green sweatshirt. It was now midafternoon, and they hadn't seen each other since he'd left her in the tree house at dawn.

She eyed the rack of dumbbells and weighted plates. "Am I allowed in here?"

"I'll take my chances." Though **after** the way he'd treated her that morning, maybe **he shoul**d reconsider.

He continued raising and lowering the barbell, feeling her eyes on his back the whole time.

"Military presses," she observed. "You can take the boy out of the army, but..."

He lost count of the repetitions, but his shrieking deltoids knew when he'd reached his limit. As he strained to raise the barbell one last time, she crossed to stand in front of him, waggling the plastic water bottle he'd brought down with him.

"Open up."

Elbows locked over his head, he growled, "Move." He couldn't put down the bar till she did. And she knew it.

"Come on." Smiling sweetly, she aimed the nozzle. "You've *gotta* be thirsty."

Arms trembling precariously, he opened his mouth like a baby bird and she filled it with a stream of cool water, grinning triumphantly. "Now, isn't that bet—"

He spewed the water into her face with the force of a geyser. She yelped and jumped back.

He let the bar down in a controlled drop to the accompaniment of her spontaneous laughter, muffled by the towel she'd grabbed to wipe her face. A smile tugged at his own lips. He'd known her reaction would be helpless mirth rather than outrage. She had the delightful capacity to laugh at her foibles and take a joke. It was one of the many surprising things he'd learned about her.

His smile faded. After his crude accusation in the sunroom that morning—and the cruder way he'd tried to demonstrate his point—he could only marvel that she was able to stomach his presence at all. He knew that in those few magic moments before he'd turned on her, she'd felt the same closeness he had, the same rightness, the same poignant beauty and fiery longing.

His gut twisted in shame when he recalled the stark pain in her eyes, the desperation that had sent her fleeing into the storm. Seeing Lugh's tattoo had triggered his suspicions, but that was no excuse for what he'd done.

She finished drying her face, her expression subdued, as if she'd read his thoughts. After an awkward silence she said, "When did Natasha have her kittens?"

"About noon. I heard these strange noises coming from under the back porch and I went to investigate. Two of the kittens had already been born."

She sat on the padded-vinyl exercise bench. "I counted four. Did you play kitty midwife?"

"Let's say I provided moral support." He paused. "You're not saying I told you so," he observed. She raised her eyebrows. "About bringing the damn things in the house." Caleb had transferred the mother and her brood to a padded cardboard box in the kitchen.

"I don't have to say I told you so," she said, with a funny little smile. "I think you knew Natasha had you beat all along."

And maybe Elizabeth knew him better than he wanted her to.

Her attention strayed to the bench she was sitting

on, with its vertical posts at the head to support a barbell. "You gonna do some bench presses? Pump up those pathetically flabby pecs?" He saw her teasing smile falter as she took in the red welts and scrapes from his earlier encounter with the tree.

Bench presses were out of the question. Considering how much weight he pressed off his chest, he'd need a spotter to do them safely—someone to stand ready to catch the bar in case he got tired and accidentally dropped it over his throat.

"I'll spot you," she said, her stare direct.

He stared back, keeping his expression carefully neutral. "No, thanks. I did some flyes and pullovers with the dumbbells. That'll take care of the pecs."

"You know there's no substitute for bench presses. Bet you haven't done them in a while, either, working out all by your lonesome down here. Come on." With an imperious little pat to the bench, she commanded him to lie down, then rose and positioned herself at the head near the bar supports.

Just his luck to kidnap a woman who knew her way around a weight room. Refusing her offer would be tantamount to saying, *I don't trust you.*

He couldn't have said why he was loath to send that message, when he'd already made it abundantly clear he *didn't* trust her. Hadn't he locked away all the dangerous household objects? What had changed since then?

Too much.

Not enough.

What the hell, he thought, crouching to change the

plates on the barbell. He'd never come close to dropping the damn thing anyway. Placing the bar in the supports, he lay back on the narrow bench with his legs braced on either side and looked at her upside down.

"Ready when you are," she said.

Caleb reached up and positioned his gloved hands on the bar, then lifted it from its brackets. Slowly he lowered it to his chest and pushed it back up, concentrating on working his pectorals, feeling them jump and twitch. He was careful to keep his movements smooth and controlled, to inhale on the down movement and exhale on the up.

"You've got good form," she said, but it was *her* form he was remembering, naked and rain-slick and wrapped around him, her hair lying wet and bedraggled over her full breasts...her slippery, tight opening stretching around his—

Enough! All he had on was a thin pair of gym shorts. Besides, pitching a tent would only steal vital blood flow from the task at hand.

She said, "Why are you smiling?"

"Just concentrating on form, sweetheart."

He finished the first set, replaced the barbell in its brackets and lay there stretching his arms and shaking them out. He noticed her faded, pine green leggings with a pinhole in the knee.

Offhandedly he said, "Next time I go into town I'll pick you up some new clothes."

"No." Her voice was flat, her features hard. "I won't accept anything from you."

In a heartbeat, the world swooped into keen-edged clarity, reminding him that she wasn't here by choice, that nothing *had* changed between them.

He could have kicked himself for thoughtlessly trampling her pride, when it was obvious she was embarrassed by her shabby wardrobe. And this definitely wasn't the time to make such an offer, on the heels of this morning's encounter, when it could be misconstrued as payment for services almost rendered. If he'd thought she'd been after David's money, one look at her face right now was enough to obliterate any such notion.

Feeling heat rush to his face, he said, "I just meant..."

Oh hell. He settled back on the bench and concentrated on his second set of presses.

She said, "When you *do* go into town, are you going to handcuff me again?"

"No," he answered without hesitation. He'd made that decision the instant his Land Rover broke down on his way home from the supermarket four days ago. Hour after interminable hour, as he'd waited for the tow truck, then harangued, threatened and cajoled the overworked mechanic, all he could think of was Elizabeth helplessly shackled to the daybed. What if he *had* been lying unconscious somewhere? The horrible truth was, no one would have known she was there. It was an unacceptable risk, and one he refused to take again. If anything had happened to her...

He couldn't recall ever feeling this protective of anyone, not since his mother. Of course, his feelings for Elizabeth were in a different league altogether. And far too complex for comfort.

When he started the third set of bench presses, her stance changed subtly, her hands hovering near the bar. His gaze lingered on her knuckles, scraped as raw as his chest and arms. Puffing with exertion, he grunted, "Damn tree."

A hint of a smile. "Don't talk. Breathe."

"Yes, Coach."

When he started to slip the bar back into its brackets, she said, "I know you can do one more."

He wasn't so sure. His muscles felt as wobbly and weak as those newborn kittens upstairs. He took in her alert stance, her confident expression. Urging him to push himself to the limit.

"Don't worry," she said. "I'm right here."

Unbidden memories swamped him...of her clinging to him, ready to give herself to him. *I could never hurt you*, he'd told her, and she'd believed him. Trusted him. Yielded to him as she'd never yielded to another.

And now she was asking him to trust her.

Damn it, he could bull through one more bench press. Struggling to maintain his breathing, he lowered the bar to his chest and huffed as he slowly raised it. Before she could grab it and slide it back onto the supports, he started lowering it again, his eyes burning into hers, wondering if he'd lost his mind. Whatever happened to him at this point was his own miserable fault.

On the down movement he thought he was going to

lose it. His eyes squeezed shut and she talked him through it, her encouraging tone of voice registering more than the words. A bark of exertion escaped him as he pushed the bar off his chest, his entire body vibrating with the effort.

His eyes creaked open and homed in on those scraped knuckles inches above his face, her hands poised under the bar as it slowly rose. When his arms were fully extended she helped him roll it onto the brackets. Never had anything sounded as sweet as the solid clang when the bar settled in place, rocking the bench.

She folded her arms on the bar and shared his breathless chuckle. Had he ever felt this connected to anyone? If so, he couldn't recall. Lazily, his overstressed arms trembling, he reached up and drew her fingers down. He pressed his lips to those abused knuckles.

He murmured, "You'd have made a hell of a drill sergeant, Elizabeth."

Her smile melted away. When she just studied him solemnly, he sat up and leaned on a palm, letting his expression do the asking. *What did I say?*

She whispered, "You called me Elizabeth."

He blinked, trying to remember when he'd last thought of her as Lizzie. "I did, didn't I?" he murmured.

She caught her bottom lip between her teeth, her eyes soul-dark and suspiciously shiny. He was astounded. Such a little thing—calling her what she'd asked to be called—and yet it meant so much to her.

His stubborn refusal to grant her that simple courtesy must have seemed hopelessly petty and mean-spirited.

Hell, he thought, it *was* petty and mean-spirited. Just one more way to grind her down, to underscore her powerlessness.

What kind of man was he?

She offered a lopsided smile. "It won't work, you know. I'm not going to stop calling you Rambo."

"Hey, it was worth a try." He stripped off his gloves, reached for the towel on the floor and started wiping down his face and chest. He said quietly, "I didn't expect you to come looking for me today, af-ter...everything. I figured you'd be busy putting a razor edge on your fingernails."

A touch of sadness crept into her eyes. He reached out to stroke her cheek and cup her face in his palm. He felt her swallow, felt the tightness in her throat. She asked, "Why did you stop?"

He didn't have to ask, *Stop what?* He drew a long, slow breath and slid his hand down to clasp hers. "You...surprised me. I didn't realize you were a virgin." She opened her mouth. "Don't say it. I know. I didn't believe you."

A cold ball of apprehension settled in his stomach. What else had she been telling the truth about?

Damn his brother. David had misled him—at least with respect to one critical little detail! Caleb tried to fit in Elizabeth's lack of sexual experience with the predatory image David had drawn. Could she have been simply guarding her virginity for a worthier prospect?

Even as the ugly rationalization took shape, he jettisoned it. That kind of cold calculation may have jibed with the woman Caleb had expected when he'd engineered this mission, but it had nothing to do with the woman he'd come to know since. Still, he couldn't dismiss his brother's pain, his impassioned recounting of the treatment he'd suffered at her hands.

Who was he to believe? David or Elizabeth? Or did the truth lie somewhere in between?

She looked away and then back at him, high color blossoming in her cheeks. "But even so, you knew I didn't want you to stop."

"Elizabeth." He squeezed her hand. "That was the hardest thing I've ever done, walking away from you this morning. But I had to. You're under my protection."

"*Protection!*" She snatched her hand away. "How chivalrous. Most people call it unlawful imprisonment."

"Call it what you will, it boils down to one thing— while you're here, I'm responsible for you. For providing for your needs and keeping you safe. And that sure as hell doesn't include..." *Making sweet, deep, scorching love to you till your head and heart and body are filled with nothing but me.*

He cleared his throat. "This morning was...a mistake. I never should have let things get so out of hand. It won't happen again." After an uncomfortable silence he said, "I thought twenty-five-year-old virgins were an extinct species."

She shrugged and circled the exercise bench to sit next to him, facing the opposite direction. "What can I tell you? We're making a comeback."

"What is it, AIDS? The whole safe-sex thing?"

"That's part of it. The only safe sex is no sex, right? But there's more to it than that. At least for me. I always figured...well, making love is the most intimate experience you can share with anyone. Why squander it—cheapen it—by doing it with someone you don't really care for?"

Her explanation lingered in the silence that followed, along with its inescapable corollary: Elizabeth cared for him. Enough to give herself to him in this most intimate way. That knowledge thrilled him on a gut-deep level when he knew he ought to be dismayed.

He asked, "How did you survive three weeks at Avalon, uh...intact?"

With a sneer of distaste she said, "That Lugh's a piece of work. He came on to me, pretty brazenly, the first day I was there."

"Were you surprised?"

"I was, yes. I knew they discourage that kind of thing at Avalon. Free love has no place in their communal philosophy. It's all about the rhythms of nature and good hard work, mainly farming."

"And scrubbing latrines."

She grimaced at the reminder. "That's the job they give new people. You've gotta work your way up to tilling the good earth. Of course, there's a lot of harmony-and-love stuff, too, but strictly the platonic variety."

"So the sexual revolution kinda got left back in the sixties."

"I guess so. They're pretty conservative that way. Besides, everyone works so hard, they're too exhausted for sex. The closest they get to physical intimacy is a group hug each morning."

"So how did you discourage Lugh? I understand he can be pretty persistent."

"Well, of course, I told him I'm a virgin. I thought that would be the end of it, that he'd respect my inexperience and leave me alone."

"Let me guess. He was more turned on than ever."

"How'd you know?"

"Shot in the dark." Caleb smiled at her naiveté.

"He was...intrigued by my innocence. That's how he put it. Anyway, he made it clear, in that smooth-talking way he has, that sleeping with him was part of the deal. He wasn't going to back down."

"And yet he must have."

"Well, see, he's really into this cycles-of-nature business. Everything revolves around the lunar calendar. According to Lugh, the ideal time for me to yield the, uh, closed bud of my innocence and enter the full flower of womanhood blah blah blah was during the next full moon—that being the most auspicious time for any kind of change or transition."

"Lucky for you, I got you out of there before he had a chance to pluck your bud." So this was what she'd been talking about the night of her migraine, when she'd sat in the bathtub staring at the skylight. His temples throbbed with a surge of blood pressure. "So you were actually going to let him—"

"No! Good grief, Caleb, what do you think? I was going to leave before then. Then return after the full moon."

"Fiendishly clever," he said, with more than a touch of sarcasm.

She slumped. "It was the only thing I could think of."

"Did you give them all your money?" he asked.

"Yep. Wiped out my bank account." She had her hands stuffed in that kangaroo pocket, staring straight ahead with a rueful half smile. "All three hundred sixteen bucks and nineteen cents."

For a moment he thought she had to be kidding. Then he abruptly turned away.

As if sensing his discomfort, she said quietly, "It's been a lean year for work."

Clearly an understatement. "And you let them tattoo you."

She shrugged. "Hey, you only live once, right?"

He looked at her. "Tell me why you joined."

She met his gaze, their faces inches apart. Her eyes weren't simply brown, as he'd thought. There was a ring of amber in the center of the iris, which expanded now as he watched, mesmerized.

She said, "You're ready to hear this?"

"Just lay it on me before I change my mind."

She took a deep breath. "David called me from Avalon. He was real furtive, kind of whispering."

"What did he say?"

"He was terrified. Something was going on that he couldn't tell me about over the phone. He only said he didn't want to end up like Tessa."

"Who's Tessa?"

"I didn't know at the time, but later I found out she was another member who quit the commune about the time David died. Anyway, he begged me to help him—to do what, I don't know, but he made me promise to meet him the next day. Said he'd try to slip away for a couple of hours. Of course, I agreed. He was..." She bit her lip. "You should've heard him."

Caleb didn't have to. He'd heard the same fear and desperation in his brother's voice when David had called to ask him to keep Elizabeth safe. But David hadn't said anything about Tessa or any nefarious goings-on.

Caleb rested his elbows on his knees and thrust his fingers through his sweat-damp hair. "If David had thought something was fishy at Avalon, he would've asked *me* to help him, not you. I'm the logical choice. I'm trained for that sort of thing."

"Maybe it's like I said before. He just couldn't face your disapproval, knowing how you felt about the commune. If he'd asked for your help, you'd have probably found out he'd joined because he wanted to."

"I'll never believe that. No one forced him into it,

that's true, but he was compelled to by...by circumstances."

"Those circumstances being the way I treated him. Say what you mean, Caleb." She stared him down, with the righteous indignation of the unjustly maligned.

"All right, yes. By the way you treated him." That hadn't been so hard to say a couple of weeks ago. "So did you meet with him?" he asked.

"No. He died that night." A heavy silence followed, until she asked, "Do you want to hear why *I* think he joined?"

"Why not?"

"I figure it was a combination of factors, the first being David's mental outlook. He was never a happy person. Never had confidence in himself or his ability to cope with the day-to-day challenges and decisions all of us have to face. Tell me that's not true."

It was true. Caleb waved her on.

"The communal life-style is very seductive for that type of person," she continued, "almost a return to the carefree days of childhood. Think about it. All your decisions are made for you. Where you live. What kind of work you do. What you eat. When you wake up and when you go to bed. You give up your freedom of choice, but in return you get security, support, approval."

He couldn't deny David would have been drawn to that kind of life. "What else?"

"I'm pretty sure Lugh sniffs out the more affluent

prospective members and takes extra pains to recruit them."

"You won't get an argument from me on that."

One dark eyebrow rose. "Wonders never cease."

"I don't know, Elizabeth. Somehow I can't see a sensitive artist type like my brother swabbing out urinals."

"Some members have special skills that are of use to the commune. Bookkeeping, cooking, what have you. Then they're exempt from the regular chores."

"But a graphic artist?" David must've scoured a lot of porcelain those last few weeks.

"That's the funny thing. I asked around about David when I was there—subtly, of course. He never worked in the latrines. Or in the fields or the kitchen or any of the public areas. They had him doing something—I don't know—classified. He never talked to anyone about it."

Caleb felt the buzz of adrenaline in his veins.

Something classified.

What had they had his little brother doing at Avalon?

Elizabeth said, "Just like you, I'm acting on a vow I made to David. I promised to help him—" her voice cracked "—and I was too late."

Caleb laid a hand on her shoulder, moved by her impotent grief, which mirrored his own. "Elizabeth..." He almost said, *It's not your fault,* but didn't that go against everything he'd believed since his brother's death? Ultimately, if even a fraction of what

David had told him about their relationship was true, then his brother's tragic fate was indeed her fault.

Caleb squeezed her shoulder and said, "You agreed to meet him. What more could you have done?"

With a helpless shake of her head she said, "I—I could've called the police. Told them I thought something suspicious was going on."

"On the basis of that one phone call? They would've laughed. The cops won't go near Avalon, not without a damn good reason. Lugh has courted all the local politicos. Made hefty contributions to a few campaign funds."

"I just feel like I should've done *something*. I owed him that much. We were so close, for so long, David and I. Even through the strain of his romantic attachment to me, we remained friends. After he died, I figured the only way I could fulfill my promise to help him was to infiltrate the commune myself and investigate his death. I had to wait a few weeks till I'd finished some work I'd already committed to. Then I told my agent I'd be off the scope for a while and I joined Avalon."

"And brought along that little semiautomatic in case things got hairy."

"That's right."

"Do you know how to use it?"

Her long-suffering look spoke volumes.

He said, "Okay, stupid question."

As one of the best marksmen in the world, Caleb admitted to a certain arrogance in this department. Firearm skills were at the core of the Delta Force training program. He'd spent hours each day refining esoteric shooting techniques, firing hundreds of rounds at a time till his trigger finger seized up.

He could walk into a room where innocent people were being held and, in a split second, identify and shoot the terrorists before they had a chance to kill their hostages. It wasn't a job for the average soldier.

She said, "I do target shooting. I'm a pretty good shot. That gun's licensed."

"Do you have a carry permit?"

She smirked. "Is the kidnapper threatening to turn me in for carrying a concealed weapon?"

He ignored that one. "Weren't you concerned that David might have told Lugh about you? That he'd recognize your name?"

"I told them I'm a secretary and I used the name Beth. And my mother's maiden name, Russell."

"What else did you find out while you were at Avalon?"

She sighed. "Not bloody much, as Lugh would say. They kept me pretty busy, as you know, but I managed to snoop around a little. *Something's* going on. People coming and going at odd hours. A lot of closed-door meetings in the administration building. Lugh had me living there, in a room in his private apartments. Didn't want me bunking in one of the cabins, where someone might beat him to..."

"Your bud?"

She smirked again.

"So you were there for three weeks," he said, "right in the heart of the operation, but you still couldn't come up with anything more incriminating than a few secret meetings. Maybe they were deciding how much toilet paper to buy."

"Caleb, something's going on there! My instincts were screaming the whole time."

"The only thing Lugh's guilty of is targeting well-heeled, emotionally needy recruits and forcing them to turn over their assets. Plus his questionable political influence. The guy's sleazy, I'll grant you, but you're not going to convince me he's responsible for David's suicide."

"I don't think it was suicide. I think he uncovered some kind of criminal activity and they murdered him."

She was only voicing his initial suspicions, but he shook his head. "Ridiculous."

"Caleb, did David ever seem suicidal to you? He wasn't the happiest person, it's true, but did you ever know him to be seriously depressed?"

"Not before you." When she failed to respond, he said, "I can't ignore the things he told me. He couldn't have made it all up."

Maybe she wasn't the irredeemable witch he'd originally thought, but at the very least, she'd been callous and insensitive to David's strong feelings for her.

Wearily she asked, "Do you at least believe me about why I joined?"

"Yes. But you're on the wrong track. David killed himself. I would have known if he'd been in danger," Caleb said tightly.

"Why?"

He clenched his fists. "I just know I would have. Something would've clued me in."

It *couldn't* have been murder. Caleb was one of a handful of the most superbly trained warriors in the world. Surely he would have known if his own brother had been at risk from outside forces. No, the only risk to David had come from himself, from his own weakness and inability to cope with Elizabeth's rejection—something Caleb couldn't have foreseen or prevented.

She said quietly, "Now who's feeling guilty?" When he remained silent, she touched his arm. "David was his own man, Caleb. You aren't responsible for what happened to him any more than I am."

"He was...weak."

"And you blame the fact that you weren't around during his adolescence."

Was he that transparent? "Our dad died when he was only two," he said. "I should've made sure he grew up stronger." ·

"That was your mother's job, not yours. If anyone's at fault, it's her. How old was he when you left for West Point?"

"Just ten."

She paused. "That's how old you were when you lost your father, no?"

"Yeah."

"Who was *your* male role model?" He didn't answer. "You didn't have one. But you managed to grow up secure and self-reliant."

He snorted. "I didn't have much choice. You never

met my mother." He scrubbed the back of his neck and closed his eyes on the memories. "When Dad died, everyone told me, 'You're the head of the family now, son. You've gotta take care of your mother.'"

"That's a stupid and thoughtless thing to tell a young boy," Elizabeth snapped, rising to the defense of the confused, grief-stricken child he'd been. "That's the sort of thing people say when they're uncomfortable, groping for words."

"Only in this case it was true. Mom was...well, she was timid. Introverted. She couldn't handle things on her own, so I had to grow up fast. I took on a lot of responsibility, but someone had to do it."

"But don't you see? David was the same age when he lost you. When you joined the army. Chances are, he would've developed the same whether you'd been there or not. People are born different. Maybe he just had more of your mother in him than you did."

Caleb looked into her eyes, staggered by the depth of emotion he read there. Her sincerity. Her impulse to comfort and reassure him. And underlying it all, her indisputable strength of character.

This scrappy, strong-willed woman couldn't have had much in common with his brother. He wondered about the forces that had shaped her. "What about you?" he asked. "When did you lose your parents?"

She blinked. "My parents aren't dead." She must have seen the shock in his eyes. "Is that what David told you?"

"He said you're all alone, that you have no one else

to look after you." As if she needed someone to look after her!

"Well, that's true enough. I haven't been in touch with my folks in years."

"Not at all?"

She hesitated, and he wondered what was under the rock he'd just turned over.

"They divorced when I was a baby," she said. "It was a shotgun wedding anyway—my mom was pregnant with me." He felt her stiffen. "Most divorced people fight over who gets to keep the children. They fought over who had to *take* me, and I kind of got shuttled between them. They both remarried and started having more kids. *Real* kids, the kind that are planned. I was like this fifth wheel no one particularly wanted around."

Caleb squeezed the edge of the bench to keep from hauling her into his arms. She didn't want his pity. He growled, "Sounds like you were raised by a couple of shallow, selfish jerks."

Her voice tight with bitterness, she said, "Mystery solved. Now you know how I ended up like that."

His breath snagged. "God, Elizabeth. That's not what I meant." And yet hadn't he made it clear that's precisely what he thought of her? He studied her tense features as she stared at the floor.

He said quietly, "You know, we're alike in a way. We're both loners. Maybe it was the way we were raised, I don't know. We don't like to rely on anyone else."

She looked up, but not at him. "Tell me why you quit the army, Caleb."

He slung the towel over the back of his neck. "It'd been creeping up on me for a while. The—" he shrugged "—disillusionment."

"Disillusionment with what? The violence?"

He paused, trying to articulate what had made him turn his back on soldiering, the only life he knew. "It's not the violent life-style per se as much as how it changes you. I guess I just decided I didn't want to lose any more of the man I'd been before." He looked at her. "Does that make sense?"

He could see her thinking about it. When she said, "Yes," he believed her.

"And then I lost both David and Mom, within such a short period of time, and that kind of clinched it. In my gut I knew it was time to start over."

"Do you regret it?"

"Not yet. Maybe I will someday."

"How did you get the scars?" She peered around him to look at the arm farthest from her, with its jagged pink line snaking up to the shoulder.

Absently he rubbed the matching scar on his temple. "You don't want to hear about that."

"Probably not, but tell me anyway."

He glanced at her obdurate expression. "It happened years ago, during an operation to rescue an American businessman with CIA connections. He was being held in a Central American prison, guarded by men with orders to kill him if we tried to get him out. As the demolitions expert, I blasted us through a cupola in the roof. Then we made our way down to the cell where the hostage was being held, put some Kevlar body armor on him and took him back up to a waiting helicopter."

"Didn't the guards try to stop you?"

"Yes."

Her face lost some color, and she glanced briefly at his hands before looking away. His hands, which had caressed her so intimately just hours ago. They'd also done their share of killing.

He said matter-of-factly, "They tried to stop us and we killed them. Except there was this one guy who didn't put up a fight. He was shaking like a leaf—cowering on the stairs as we made our way down. I handcuffed him to the banister."

Caleb didn't relish those memories, but he didn't hide from them, either. He'd been a professional warrior, like countless men before him. "A few of us were hanging off the helicopter pods when it was shot down," he said, indicating the scars. "A couple of my buddies were hurt worse. We surrounded the chopper and returned a lot of rifle fire before an armored personnel carrier stormed through to get us out."

"Was the hostage okay?"

"Not a scratch."

Caleb sat facing away from her, feeling her eyes on him. Finally she reached across his chest and laid her cool fingers on his upper arm, on the ugly, twisting scar. She leaned against his other arm. He hadn't realized till that instant that he'd been holding his breath. He laid his own hand on hers, and they sat like that for several minutes.

That businessman he'd helped rescue in Central America had been the focus of a mission; he'd never meant anything to Caleb personally. That was how he wanted to feel about Elizabeth. How he wished he could feel about her.

"Caleb." She waited till he'd turned his full attention to her. "You know now that I wasn't a real member of the commune." She studied his expression, and he saw the instant her hopes deflated. "You're still not going to let me go, are you?" she whispered.

"No, Elizabeth. I'm not."

She turned from him, and he put a hand on her shoulder. She jerked away and stood up.

"And you know why," he said. "This doesn't change the promise I made to David. If you're right and there's something dirty going on at Avalon, you're in even more danger as an infiltrator than if you were a real member."

He didn't tell her the rest of it. That he cared about her safety on a personal level that had nothing to do with David or any vow. He wished he could worry about her with his head only, not his gut. Or his heart.

But it was already too late for that.

7

THE SOFT EDGES of sleep burned away like fog. Caleb shifted restlessly on his bed. He'd been dreaming. Something about his hand. Even now he absently rubbed the back of his right hand as the dream sensations coalesced into something his waking mind recognized.

Pain.

Groggily he sat up and swung his feet to the floor. Groped for the lamp switch and shoved his hair out of his eyes. Blinked in the glare and was suddenly wide-awake, staring at the back of his right hand.

He'd seen this before—years ago, when he was training at Fort Bragg, North Carolina, the headquarters for Special Forces. Then, as now, he hadn't felt the spider bite. When his allergic reaction had kicked in several hours later, it was just like this—a hot, itchy, bull's-eye swelling, white ringed with red, with a dark blister at the center. About the size of a half-dollar.

It must have happened just before dinner while he was cleaning out the shed, preparing it for winter tool storage. Well, at least he remembered what to do about it. Yawning, scratching his hand, he grabbed the key ring from under his pillow and headed down the hall. He wore only an undershirt and gray sweatpants, and the late October chill raised goose bumps on his bare arms.

He passed Elizabeth's closed door and wondered which naughty nightie she was wearing, what position she was sleeping in. He pictured her sprawled alluringly with one arm flung over her head and one knee bent. She'd tossed off her covers and her full breasts rose and fell slowly under thin, ice blue silk. She murmured something in her sleep, her lips parting.... She was dreaming about him, about the tree house....

Softly cursing his reckless imagination, he padded down the stairs. The last week since the Tree-House Incident had been tougher to get through than Delta training. He'd assumed that the more time he and Elizabeth spent together, the less he'd ache to finish what he'd started on that rainy morning. Wasn't familiarity supposed to breed, if not contempt, then at least disinterest?

Instead each passing day installed her more firmly in his life and under his skin. And made him crave her with an intensity he'd never experienced before, not even in the hormone-saturated throes of adolescence.

In the last few weeks he'd learned how to coax that sweet, lopsided smile from her...how to read her body language and know when she needed space. He looked forward to the simple things they did together, from their morning runs to playing with Natasha's kittens, raking leaves, stargazing with his telescope and playing Scrabble by toasty firelight on his den's flagstone hearth.

And every night he lay awake remembering that storm-ravaged dawn, her sleepy look of desire, the way she'd panted softly and shivered at his touch. Remembering the feel of her hot body in his arms as he'd stood in the icy drizzle under the trapdoor, pressing into her slick heat.

Vivid memories of the last part—the teeth-grinding struggle to derail his raging need at the very threshold of penetration—helped Caleb keep their interactions from becoming too cozy and intimate. He knew he could never walk away from her a second time.

Downstairs, he unlocked the door to the "chamber of horrors," the storage room off the kitchen, and rummaged through the paper sack of goodies he'd swept out of the medicine chest three weeks earlier. Aspirin, cough syrup, razors, assorted lotions and potions of his mother's... There it was, a box of over-the-counter antihistamine tablets.

He opened the box and pulled out the one remaining blister-pack card. The foil backing was riddled with holes where all the pills had been punched through. He shook the box. No good. Somehow it had been put away empty. He dumped the contents of the paper sack on the floor and squatted to paw through the jumble of bottles and boxes, then sat back on his heels. Nothing.

It was 2:00 a.m. As soon as the drugstore opened in the morning, he'd go out. Unfortunately, there was no such thing as a twenty-four-hour pharmacy or convenience store in this remote area.

He examined his right hand and frowned. The fingers had puffed up like sausages, and his forearm had begun to swell and redden, accompanied by a burning itch. Strange, he hadn't swollen up like this last time. Of course, there were spiders and then there were *spiders*. He recalled that years ago, one of the local residents had gone into anaphylactic shock following a spider bite. The poor guy hadn't even made it to the hospital.

Caleb rose and left the storage room, relocking it behind him, and made his way upstairs. Despite the cold, he was sweating, whether from his allergic reaction or nerves, he didn't know.

Elizabeth was waiting at the top of the stairs, hugging herself in that pink terry robe. A froth of ice blue silk peeked out at the hem, and he smiled despite everything.

She said, "I heard you prowling around. Anything wrong?" Her hair was a mess, her eyes sleep-squinty. She was gorgeous.

"I was just looking for something. Go back to bed." He started past her.

"Caleb!" She grabbed his puffy arm and turned it this way and that, peering at the discolored swelling on the back of his hand.

He shrugged as nonchalantly as he could. "It's just a spider bite."

He stared down at her bent head as a rush of warmth filled his chest. Her concern was spontaneous, genuine. This must be what it felt like to be coddled and cared for. He clenched the keys in his other hand to keep from stroking her hair.

She said, "You should get medical attention for this."

"It's nothing. It's happened before."

"It has?" Her worried eyes bored into his, as if to gauge his honesty. "Like this?"

"Well, not exactly like this. I'm going to get some antihistamines in the morning. That'll take care of it."

She bit her lip. "I don't know, Caleb...maybe it's like bee stings. The first exposure sensitizes you, and the next time you're in real trouble. Life-threatening trouble."

He hadn't thought of that. "Well, like I said, I'll take care of it in the morning. Go back to bed." He quickly sidestepped her, entered his own room, tossed the keys on his dresser and collapsed onto the bed.

HE JERKED AWAKE, heart slamming against his ribs. She was here, in his room. He peered into the murky shadows and found himself alone.

He took a deep breath, tried to slow his racing pulse. It had been a dream, but a vivid one. Even now, his imagination teased him with her lingering scent....

He touched his arm. The swelling now extended nearly to his shoulder, and it itched unmercifully. He was chilled and his throat felt a bit tight. Just enough to make him wonder if it was his imagination or the beginnings of a more severe reaction.

"Christ," he muttered. Could he hang on till the drugstore opened? Could he even drive in this condition? What if his throat did close up? Any other time he'd consider calling an ambulance to take him to the emergency room, just to be on the safe side, but with an unwilling houseguest in residence, that wasn't an option.

The sound of a car outside made him bolt upright. He tossed his pillow aside and groped around on the bare sheet. His keys were gone! Then he remembered tossing them on his dresser, and felt his gut clench. He stumbled to the window in time to see starlight glint off his Land Rover before it raced down the drive and out of sight. She *had* been in his room—it was no dream!

He pounded his fist against the window frame, then wished he'd chosen the other hand. Cradling his swollen arm, cursing violently, he slumped onto the bed. And almost laughed. It seemed he'd underestimated her for the last time. Any other night, his keys would have been safely tucked under his pillow; he'd have snapped awake the instant she tried to get them.

But she hadn't tried it any other night. No, she'd patiently waited to make her move—waited until he was weakened, distracted. Careless. Waited until he was, as she'd put it herself, in life-threatening trouble.

So much for the worried looks, the concerned words. Yes, her talents were definitely wasted on those sleazy commercials.

"Elizabeth," he whispered. "I really could've..."

What? *Loved you?*

He squeezed his eyes shut. The last few weeks...the sense of closeness, of companionship...

Had all been an illusion, he reminded himself brutally. How could he have thought otherwise? Nothing had ever changed between them. She'd always been his prisoner, and he'd always been her nightmare. Could he blame her for bolting at the first opportunity, after what she'd endured at his hands? The truth was, he couldn't.

Still, it hurt. More than the fear of his throat swelling shut.

He considered retrieving a phone from the storage room and calling that ambulance. Considered it for a whole two seconds before flopping back on the bed.

HE DIDN'T WANT TO LET GO of this dream. He fought the tug of wakefulness and savored the illusion of cool fingers on his brow, followed by the imprint of exquisitely soft lips. *Her* lips.

"Caleb..." she whispered.

The instant he realized he wasn't alone, his warrior's training took over. Even before his eyes opened, his hand shot out in reflex and clamped around a slender wrist.

She gasped, her brown eyes huge.

Was he still dreaming? "Elizabeth?"

"Who else would it be?" She pulled against his brutal hold. "Caleb, you're hurting me."

Only then did he realize how hard he was gripping her wrist. He let go. "You came back."

She looked nonplussed. "Of course I came back. I'm surprised you even knew I was gone. You were asleep when I left. Here, take this."

She tore open a small paper packet and helped prop him up on an elbow. He recognized the cold-and-

allergy pill she placed between his lips, a common antihistamine. She lifted a glass of water to his mouth
and he swallowed the pill.

"Better make it two," she said, tearing open another
packet.

Obediently he took it, then lay back again. She
found his pillow where he'd thrown it on the floor,
and tucked it under his head. He could only stare at
her in wonder.

He looked at the pile of single-dose packets on the
night table. "Where...?"

"I got onto the main highway and just kept driving.
I knew eventually I'd find a truck stop or an all-night
gas station that sold convenience items. Your wallet
was on the dresser. Here's the change." She reached
into her jeans pocket and dumped a few bills and
coins on the night table.

He chuckled. Resourceful as always, his Elizabeth.
He groped for her hand and squeezed it.

Her worried face hovered over him. "Are you going
to be all right?"

He nodded. *Now that you're back.*

She scowled. "I'm warning you right now, if these
pills don't do the job pronto, I'm dragging you to the
nearest emergency room. You scared the bejesus out
of me!"

"Scared me, too, sweetheart." *But not half as much as
the thought of never seeing you again.*

She dropped his keys next to the money and pill
packets, then straightened his covers, turned off the
lamp and crawled into bed next to him, fully dressed.

He said, "You don't have to—"

"I don't recall you giving me a choice when I had my migraine. That's the way it works. You're at my mercy, Rambo." She curled up against his side and slid her arm over his waist.

He grinned. The name was beginning to grow on him.

"Do you think you could eat some eggs?" Elizabeth placed a mug of coffee on the kitchen table in front of Caleb.

"I don't think so, thanks. This is enough for now."

He looked like hell. The swelling in his arm had receded, but he looked bleary and exhausted.

She sat across from him. "Did you really think I'd abandoned you?"

One broad shoulder lifted. "What can I tell you? I was delirious." Despite his light tone, he avoided her eyes.

She fiddled with her coffee cup. "I guess you and I don't know each other as well as I thought."

He sighed and leaned on his elbows, dragging all ten fingers through his rumpled hair. "Elizabeth. Did it occur to you that once I was no longer helpless, you'd be at my mercy again?"

"Yes. Did it occur to *you* that if I left you all alone, suffering a potentially fatal allergic reaction, I could never live with myself?"

"You could've tossed those pills at me and taken off again. You could've stayed away and called an ambulance. What happened to all those threats to turn me in for kidnapping?"

He sounded angry that she *hadn't* done any of those things! Was her trust misplaced? Had the gamble she'd taken backfired? Despite her misgivings, she knew that if she had it to do again, she wouldn't do anything differently.

She said, "I needed to make sure you were all right." She'd nursed him through the night, tending to him every time he woke from his restless sleep, making sure he remained medicated. "Things have changed between us, Caleb. Tell me they haven't," she challenged.

He scrubbed at his unshaven face, the whiskers rasping under his palms. He ground the sleep from his eyes and blinked. "Yes," he said hoarsely, not looking at her. "They've changed."

"Are you still going to keep me prisoner here?"

"No."

She closed her eyes and dragged in a shaky breath of relief. When she opened them, he was staring at her, his expression bleak.

"You're going to go back to Avalon, aren't you?" he asked.

"I made a promise."

"Don't do it, Elizabeth. If anything happened to you..." He didn't finish.

"Caleb, you've made good on your vow to David—"

"This isn't about David!" He lunged out of his chair and slapped his palms on the table. "This isn't about any damn vow. This is between us now. It would kill me if..." His eyelids tensed, his throat working. Quietly he finished, "If you got hurt. I'm asking you to stay, Elizabeth. You can leave anytime you want—I won't stop you. But please. Stay."

His admission, his heartfelt plea, rocked her. "I—I'll stay until you're all better," she conceded.

With a ragged sigh, he pushed himself away from the table. How long would that be? They both knew he was no longer in danger.

She said, "But you still believe the horrible things David told you about me, don't you?"

He took too long to answer. "That's in the past."

"But you believe them," she persisted.

"Elizabeth." His eyes drifted from hers. His voice sounded forced. "Maybe you didn't intend to hurt him, but you did. That's a fact. David was sensitive. He took everything too much to heart."

She pounded the table. "Dammit! I never led him on!"

"He couldn't have made it all up."

She pinned him with a cold stare. "We both know he made at least part of it up." The part about sleeping with her.

Caleb's shoulders sagged. He shook his head and murmured, "I'm beginning to wonder if I'll ever sort out this whole mess."

"Meanwhile," she said bitterly, "you may as well blame it all on me."

"I don't. Not anymore." He circled the table and stood behind her, squeezing her stiff shoulders.

"Please understand, Elizabeth. He was my brother. It's true that I didn't know him as well as I should have. But don't ask me to believe he manufactured the whole thing. He wouldn't have lied like that. Not to me."

She shook her head sadly. "What do you want from me, Caleb?"

"Time, that's all. Time to work out the answers."

Rationally she knew she couldn't expect him to simply dismiss David's story as the pack of self-serving lies it was. After all, it was a matter of his dead brother's word against that of the woman David himself had vilified.

Still, after everything she and Caleb had been through during the past weeks—and especially last night—his lack of faith was like a dagger twisting in her heart.

"ELIZABETH, COME HERE!" Caleb bellowed from the den.

Could he be having a relapse? She quickly placed little Bullwinkle—ironically, the runt of the litter—back with Natasha and the other kittens on the expensive cat bed Caleb had brought home a few days ago. He called her again, more urgently, as she sprinted into the den.

He was standing in front of the television, his eyes riveted to the screen. She started to ask him what was up, but he shushed her. A news show was on.

"...was a member of a small commune in upstate New York called the Avalon Collective. A hunter made the grisly discovery yesterday in a remote wooded area. Tessa Montgomery's decomposed body—"

Elizabeth gasped. Her thundering pulse drowned out the reporter's next words.

Caleb asked, "Didn't you say David mentioned someone named Tessa?"

She nodded woodenly. "'I don't want to end up like Tessa.' That's what he said." How many times had Elizabeth replayed that conversation in her mind, analyzing it, agonizing over what she might have done to save him?

"It has to be the same person," Caleb said. "How many Tessas can there be at Avalon?"

A photo of an attractive young woman appeared on the screen. The reporter continued, "A spokesman for the Avalon Collective tells us Miss Montgomery quit the group several months ago. Police speculate that she was murdered shortly afterward by a stranger while hitchhiking. She had apparently been bludgeoned and strangled..."

Caleb's icy calm, the rigid set of his features, made Elizabeth's pulse falter. He'd crossed some threshold, she could tell. Staring fixedly at the set, he murmured, "You really think those bastards killed my brother?"

She swallowed hard. "Yes, Caleb. I do."

"I had my doubts in the beginning that it was suicide. God, I wish I'd listened to my gut."

"It can't all be coincidence—David telling me he didn't want to end up like Tessa, at the same time she 'quit' the commune...."

"And died, supposedly the victim of random violence. Makes you wonder what he witnessed. I'd say it's a good bet she never left Avalon alive—and David didn't put that noose around his own neck."

"Maybe—maybe if I went to the police and told them what he told me—"

"Don't waste your breath. Sounds like the cops have a neat little scenario already worked out. Lugh must've concocted some sort of 'proof' that she walked away from the commune right before she died. And the politicians on his payroll will no doubt help smooth things over for him." Caleb never took his eyes off the TV screen, where Tessa Montgomery's smiling face seemed to plead for justice.

"Now do you see why I have to go back?" Elizabeth asked.

The reporter wrapped up the story and started yammering about insurance legislation. Caleb switched off the set but stood staring at the blank screen. Finally he said, "No. You're staying here. I'm going."

"*What?*"

"It's too dangerous for you. I'm trained for operations like this. I can get in, find out what's going on and get out. Then we can go to the police, once we have something to show them."

"Caleb, it won't work. Whatever's going on there, it's too well hidden. I was there for three weeks and I still couldn't put my finger on anything concrete."

"Are there locked rooms at Avalon?"

"Of course. Lots of them."

"That settles it. I can get past locks, guards, security systems. You'd just be in the way."

"What you're suggesting doesn't make sense," she argued. "I'm no lock expert, but some of those in the administration building look state-of-the-art. Unpickable."

He shrugged. "You forget, I know how to make things go boom."

"You really think Lugh and his troops are just going to stand by while you blast your way through the place?"

He hesitated, and she could practically see the wheels turning in his head. Before he could gather a rebuttal, she pressed on. "I'll go back to Avalon and tell them what happened—that I was abducted by a deprogrammer. Hell, I'm sure they figured that out anyway. I'll say I escaped from you."

He was shaking his head. "Eliz—"

"Last time, I'll admit, I didn't make the swiftest spy—I didn't know what to look for, what questions to ask. But you do. You can clue me in beforehand on all that stuff. Then, when I have the proof—"

"Whoa. You're getting ahead of yourself. Just how are you going to get this proof, with everything behind locked doors?" When she didn't answer, Caleb added, "That's where I come in."

Their gazes collided as the hard truth sank in: they needed each other to make this mission work. Neither could do it alone.

He said, "Well, if we're going to do this, let's not waste any time."

"Tomorrow's ideal."

"Why? No full moon?" One dark eyebrow rose.

She smirked. "Well, there is that. But there's an even better reason. Are you forgetting what day tomorrow is?"

He frowned. His eyes widened. "Halloween!"

"They're planning to really do it up, some kind of pagan-style celebration. A rare break from the usual drudgery. There'll be costumes, dancing, even a bonfire. And while all that's going on—"

"They just might neglect security." He pulled her into his arms.

"We can hope."

Elizabeth clung to Caleb, taking comfort from his warmth and strength. With this man as her ally, how could she fail? This was the first time they'd held each other since the Tree-House Incident a week ago. That thought seemed to occur to him, too, as he stared intently into her eyes, tightening his embrace. He stroked her hair and whispered, "You don't have to do this, Elizabeth. I wish you'd let me handle it."

"I'm going back there, Caleb, with or without you. It's something I have to finish. Please understand."

"I do understand. I just..." He sighed in resignation and dropped a whisper-soft kiss on her lips.

Suddenly all business, he barked, "I'll tell you exactly what to say and what to look for. You will follow my instructions to the letter!"

She smiled. "Yes sir, Captain Trent."

8

THE RASP OF CALEB'S fingers raised gooseflesh on Elizabeth's skin as he drew the blue bandanna around her throat. He tucked it under the collar of the oversize navy peacoat he'd given her and knotted it.

"You're trembling," he said, searching her eyes, his own glowing silver in the dim interior of the storage garage on the outskirts of the Avalon compound. It was midafternoon. They'd just slipped through the woods from the road and Caleb had made short work of the padlock on the door. They were about a quarter mile from the administration building where Lugh lived and worked.

She shrugged. "It's cold." It wasn't *that* cold, and she hoped he couldn't tell how scared she was.

He stuffed the tails of the bandanna into the open collar of her flannel shirt and snugged the jacket around her neck. "Elizabeth, I've been on too many dangerous missions not to recognize fear when I see it. You've got a right to be scared. It's not too late to back out."

She started to speak and he pressed his fingers to her lips, saying, "I won't think any less of you."

She took a deep breath. "I'm okay. Really."

For about the dozenth time, he patted the jacket pocket where she'd tucked her semiautomatic.

"It's still there," she said with a shaky chuckle.

He tilted her chin, forcing her to look him in the eye. "Remember. You're *not going to do anything risky.* Just look around, like I instructed you. If you find anything intriguing, *leave it alone and let me deal with it.* You got that?"

She nodded, afraid to speak around her chattering teeth.

He studied her face intently. "I mean it, Elizabeth. Wait for me. Now; what time are you going to meet me?" he quizzed.

"Ten p.m."

"Where?"

"Right here."

He lifted her wrist and checked her watch—again—making sure it was synchronized with his. She wasn't the only one who was nervous, but she knew his fear was for her safety, not his own.

She suppressed a shiver and peered at her surroundings. A grimy riding mower shared the garage with stacks of dirty resin chairs, an outboard motor, boat cushions and gardening and sports equipment. An enormous, tangled heap of tennis and volleyball nets occupied a nearby corner. Rakes, shovels and other tools hung from rusty hooks on the plank walls. Above their heads, perched on the rafters, were an inverted rowboat, an inflatable dinghy and some oars. The stained cement floor was littered with dried leaves that had blown in.

Caleb knelt and opened his rucksack. "Okay, let's check out my bag of tricks." He hauled out what appeared to be black binoculars with rubber eyecups and a single long scope in front. He set them aside.

"Think they'll go with my outfit?" she asked.

"These are night-vision goggles, and they're for me. I intend to keep a close eye on things. But even with these, I'll probably have trouble distinguishing you at a distance in the dark. That's why you're going to carry this."

He held out his palm, on which rested a small black box. She took it and turned it over in her hand. It was a couple of inches long and less than an inch thick. It had a three-position button and a little red eye.

She said, "Okay, I give up."

He rose. "It's a Firefly. An infrared marking beacon. Pretty simple, actually." He took it from her and briefly slid out the nine-volt battery, which just fit inside the casing. "It works like a TV remote control. Sends out an infrared signal that's invisible to the naked eye."

She was catching on. Indicating the goggles, she said, "But with these ugly suckers..."

"With these I'll see a steady light that'll help me locate you. Now, if you get in trouble—*if you need me for any reason*—just push the button to the top position, like this." He demonstrated. "Then the light will flash and I'll come right away."

"Where's the best place to hide it?" She followed the direction of his gaze. "My *bra?*"

"Trust me, your, uh, charms are more than adequate to the task."

"But how will you be able to see the signal if it's under—"

"It'll go right through your clothing. You might want to keep your jacket open, is all."

"What's this thing usually used for?"

"For identifying one's own men in the field. The range is virtually unlimited, but you've gotta be in line of sight. Outdoors, with no buildings or anything between you and the woods."

She asked, "Is that where you'll be? The woods?"

"Yep. I'll skulk around, find the best spot to observe the compound."

She smiled crookedly. "You can always climb a tree."

His eyes flashed to hers at this reference to the Tree-House Incident. The garage suddenly grew a few degrees warmer. His slow smile pierced the gloom and shot the mercury up higher still. When he started unbuttoning her jacket, the place became a sauna.

"Uh...what are you doing?" she asked.

"Installing this gizmo, what do you think?" He unfastened the top buttons of her flannel shirt, until the front of her lacy pink bra was exposed, along with a healthy display of cleavage. He smiled appreciatively. "Oh yeah, no problem."

With a growl of exasperation she made a grab for the Firefly, but he held it away.

"Uh-uh-uh," he admonished. "Allow the expert, sweetheart."

Expert in what? she wondered. *The equipment or the chosen hiding place?* She sucked in her breath as his warm fingers slid between her breasts, nestling the Firefly in place. He seemed in no hurry, taking his time to position the thing just so.

She scowled. "Stop that."

"What?" He was all innocence.

"You know damn well what!"

With obvious reluctance he withdrew his hand and buttoned up her shirt. "Is it uncomfortable?"

She wriggled her shoulders experimentally and did a little shimmy.

"Do that again," he said.

"Go to hell."

"There's not much doubt about that, sweetheart."

The corners of the Firefly were annoying, but it was a small price to pay for peace of mind. "I can live with it."

"Good. Can you push the button inconspicuously?"

She felt through her clothes for the switch. "Uh-huh."

He gave a little nod of approval, but the tight lines of his face betrayed his anxiety. He laid his hands on her shoulders. They felt solid and heavy and immensely reassuring. The last thing she wanted to do was walk away from the security of Caleb and make the solitary trek across the compound to Lugh.

Caleb's fingers tightened as if he, too, was afraid to break the contact. With a small shake of his head he whispered, "You're really willing to do this, aren't you? To put it all on the line. For David."

She blinked against the sudden sting of tears. "It's...too late for David. It's too late for Tessa. But maybe it's not too late for the next one. I'm scared, Caleb, I won't deny it, but if I wimp out now, I'd hate myself forever. I feel like my honor's at stake here."

His wide mouth curved up slightly. His eyes softened. "You could never lose your honor, Elizabeth. It's too much a part of what you are. I just wish..." His large, warm palms slid up to cup her face. "I wish I'd let myself see that about you from the beginning. I wish to God I'd listened to my instincts. About everything."

Her heart thumped painfully as she realized what he was saying. She'd waited so long for this moment.

His voice was hoarse. "I know the things David said about you couldn't have been...couldn't have been true." He dropped his hands and averted his eyes, but not before she saw the sheen of moisture in them. "This isn't easy for me, dammit."

She wanted to reach for him, but she stood frozen. He needed to say it. And she needed to hear it.

He faced her squarely. "I can't let you walk into whatever's waiting for you out there thinking that I have no faith in you. You have more integrity, more pure goodness, than anyone I know." He took a deep breath. "As for David's stories...well, I guess I'll never know whether he was an out-and-out liar or just deluded. It hurts to admit how little I knew him. That's not the kind of brother I wanted to be."

"Don't be so hard on yourself, Caleb. You didn't fail David. Whatever problems he had, they weren't due to anything you did or didn't do. The truth is, he was a stronger person than you're giving him credit for. Do you remember when you told me about your last conversation with him? When he said there was something he had to do?"

Caleb nodded.

"You assumed he was referring to suicide. I never believed he killed himself, and neither do you anymore. So what was it he felt he had to do? After all he'd seen, all he'd learned. What would *you* have done in his place?"

His eyes widened in comprehension. "I would've done what we're trying to do now. Find out what they're up to. Gather evidence—something to take to the authorities. You think that's what he…"

"David was no coward. He knew he was in danger—we both picked up on that. He could've fled the commune at any time. But he didn't. He stuck it out." She smiled. "David had more in common with his macho commando brother than either of us thought. He died a hero's death, Caleb."

"He did, didn't he?" Caleb shook his head, with a little smile of awe. "My baby brother." When he looked at her, she saw gratitude and wonder. "You amaze me, Elizabeth. How can you be so—so generous, so openhearted, after everything that's happened, after everything I believed about you, everything I did to you?" He took a deep breath. "I don't expect you to forgive me. Hell, I can't forgive myself."

"All that is in the past. As for forgiving you…" She felt her throat constrict around the words she didn't want to say, but had to. "I don't know if I have it in me to forgive it all, Caleb. I—I do understand why you did the things you did. Maybe that will have to be enough."

He took a step toward her, and she took one back, holding up a palm. Within three weeks this man had become her world. In his arms she'd known both profound terror and shattering intimacy. She needed time to sort out her conflicting emotions.

Swallowing back the tears that threatened, she continued, "Like I said, it's in the past. It's over."

He stood staring at her, his eyes wide and incandescent in the murky room. She saw his chest rise and fall swiftly under his black turtleneck and open, black leather jacket. After an eternity he said quietly, "I'll make it up to you."

A sob broke from her. His arms crushed her to him and she melted into his hot chest as he pressed fast, hard kisses to her hair.

"Elizabeth, I'm so sorry, so sorry." His long, powerful fingers tilted her head back and she felt his warm, satin lips on her closed eyelids, stealing her tears as they flowed, tugging at her eyelashes. He kissed her wet cheeks, hungry sucking kisses as if he couldn't get enough of her sorrow, as if, by taking her tears into himself, he could undo the hurt he'd caused her.

He tipped her head further. His moist mouth closed on the base of her throat where her pulse danced. She opened her eyes with a deep shiver and now she wasn't weeping but listening to her own panting breaths, unnaturally loud in the stillness of their hiding place. A sudden, squeezing pang of desire deep and low wrenched a moan from her. It was as if his ravenous mouth pulled at a taut string, commanding her passion like a master puppeteer.

He dragged his lips up to her ear. "I love you, Elizabeth," he whispered, and she clutched him in pure blind reflex, her fingers biting into the supple leather of his jacket. She was keenly attuned to the solid pressure of his hand gliding over her flannel-clad ribs and closing on the swell of her breast.

His lips met hers in a deep, consuming kiss. He angled his head, opened her mouth with insistent pressure. His strong, lithe tongue dipped and retreated, touched and probed. She whimpered into his mouth and clung tighter, terrified of the gnawing hunger that seemed to sink its fangs in deeper and deeper. His hand molded her breast possessively, as if stamping her with his mark. He pressed the aching peak between his fingertips and she pulled her mouth from his with a harsh gasp.

He whispered raggedly, "You'll always belong to me, Elizabeth."

He pushed her backward two stumbling steps and she felt herself fall. The soft mound of volleyball nets struck her back as Caleb's hot weight pressed her down into the nest.

He said, "If you leave me, I'll find you." He spread open her jacket and flicked her shirt buttons out of their buttonholes with startling speed. "I'll find you and I'll make it up to you, and by God, I'll make you need me as much as I need you."

She couldn't catch her breath, couldn't form a coherent thought. Automatically she pushed on his chest and started to utter some feeble protest. He thwarted her by capturing her lips with his own as his hand slid under her back to unfasten her bra.

Her nipples puckered in the chilly air as he pushed the lacy fabric aside and set the Firefly on the floor. He gazed at her. The dim light threw his features into sharp relief, making him look harder, hungrier. But his touch was infinitely delicate, a feather stroke as he traced the shape of her breasts. Her back arched and she found herself reaching for him, needing him.

He said, "I've waited so long, Elizabeth, too long. I'm out of my mind with wanting you."

"Caleb—" Her voice broke as his fingers plucked the tingling crests, a gentle rhythmic pinching that stole her breath. He held her gaze for a smoldering eternity, then lowered his mouth to her nipple. Elizabeth cried out at the sharp twinge of pleasure and threaded her fingers through his hair, whether to push him away or hold him closer, she couldn't say.

Suckling her with a force and urgency that made her mind whirl, he laced his fingers between hers and pinned her hands near her shoulders. His teeth scraped her and she moaned at the raw eroticism of it, twisting under him in helpless longing. He shifted his hard body to press her deeper into their nest of white cord, his erection throbbing against her.

He raised his head. His voice was a near growl. "Stop me now, Elizabeth."

She knew what he was saying. *Or it'll be too late.* Her hands were still pinned, but she arched up to press her lips to his. Her unspoken invitation seemed to electrify him. He hauled her to him roughly, returning her kiss with savage intensity. His shoulder holster dug into her breast, but she barely felt it.

His hold eased and he pulled back to study her face. "Nervous?"

She swallowed. "No."

He gave a soft smile. "Liar."

"Okay, maybe a little." Her voice was so faint and breathy, she barely heard it.

Grimly he perused their surroundings, their bizarre bedding. "It shouldn't be like this. Not your first time."

She clung to him. "It doesn't matter. Nothing matters except that...it's you."

Tenderly he kissed her forehead, her cheeks and finally her mouth. Rising to his knees, straddling her, he yanked off his jacket and flung it away in one movement. Next came the leather shoulder holster, which supported a big .45 semiautomatic on one side, with two spare magazines hanging under the other arm. He removed the rig and set it down within reach. He pulled off his sweater, then rose and shed the rest of his clothing, including a compact .32 semiautomatic in an ankle holster.

Naked, he knelt over her once more, the essence of masculine grace and virility. She stared in awe as soft light and shadow delineated the powerful contours of his body. His spectacularly aroused body. Seeing him like this, poised over her as if to devour her, drove home the enormity of what she was about to do. Holding her breath, she raised her eyes to his. There she read both raging need and patient tenderness as he lifted her hand and brought it to his penis.

Tentatively she touched him, this most mysterious part of him, which would soon become part of her. How different from what she'd imagined, exquisite, like marble encased in hot satin. And so alive under her hand. After a few moments his fingers abruptly clamped around her wrist as a guttural sound escaped his throat.

"I like that too much," he rasped, and pulled her to a sitting position. He made short work of her jacket, bandanna, shirt and bra. Still kneeling, he lifted her to her feet and finished undressing her till she stood naked before him. She shivered, though the fire in her veins had chased off the chill.

His hands trailed up the backs of her thighs and gripped her bottom. She felt his hot breath between her legs, followed by the scalding pressure of his mouth. Her hoarse cry bounced off the plank walls as her knees threatened to buckle. His fingers joined the assault, lazily stroking, exploring, teasing, until all she could do was clutch his hair and whimper his name.

She tensed when a finger began to slowly burrow inside. After a moment she felt her body begin to relax, and he must have felt it, too, because he pressed on then, probing gently, stretching her, a deep, relentless invasion. Vaguely, through the haze of pleasure, she realized he did this to prepare her, to make their first joining easier for her.

Her thigh muscles quivered, her breath came fast and shallow. His touch turned bolder, the rhythm faster, keeping time with her panting gasps. She was reduced to a knot of pure sensation, all slippery heat and wanting. His agile tongue found the tiny pulsing hub of that sensation, and it was too much. Reflexively she tried to twist away, but he held her tight.

Her gasps became sharp cries, matching the crescendo building in her body. *"Caleb!"*

Suddenly the room spun as he pulled her legs out from under her, catching her as she fell. Her senses reeled; she was poised on the fine edge of release, drunk with the scent of him, with the heat and weight of him crushing her down into the springy pile of nets. The steady pressure of his hard, hair-roughened thighs opened her wide.

"Elizabeth...I wanted to go slow for you. I'm trying," he said, with a breathless chuckle. "I'm trying my damnedest."

He kissed her hard, threatening her sanity with a renewed surge of pumping hunger. The restless movement of her hips was answered with a stabbing pressure as he began to flex into her. She bit back a groan. He held himself still, tight as a coiled spring, quivering with barely restrained need. "Trust me," he whispered, staring into her eyes, stroking her face with trembling fingers.

She knew he was struggling to hold back, letting her

set the pace. Trust him? She trusted him with her life. With a tremulous smile she willed the tension from her body, forcing herself to relax. She slid her hands around his waist and wordlessly urged him deeper. True to his word, he rocked into her slowly, stretching and filling her by degrees, never taking his eyes from hers.

It was too beautiful, too sweetly fulfilling; her body and soul ached for completion. With a sharp cry of pleasure and pain, she arched into him hard and they became one. Caleb groaned. His face twisted for a moment as he gathered his control, then those silver eyes seared her.

"You are so beautiful, Elizabeth. So beautiful."

He slid his fingers down her belly and caressed her as their bodies retreated and came together, dissolving her discomfort under a deluge of pure, electrifying sensation. Gradually the tempo of their loving built until they were panting, sweat-slick, moving as one.

She gasped in astonishment as her body tightened and the pinnacle came within reach. He tilted her hips and plunged with ferocious intent as her climax swelled and crested and crashed over her in scorching waves. Just when she feared she'd spiral into oblivion, she felt his strong arms wrap around her, grounding her.

Caleb's peak came fast on the heels of hers. At the last moment he withdrew and crushed her to him with a savage cry. She felt the pulsing warmth against her belly and knew he'd done this to protect her, chagrined that until that moment, birth control hadn't entered her mind.

They lay tangled, their stampeding heartbeats slowing in tandem. She stared into the rafters as he stroked her hair. She felt his eyes on her.

He whispered, "Elizabeth...?" Finally she turned to meet his warm gaze. "You okay, sweetheart?"

She smiled and nodded, and shivered as the chill of the garage cooled her damp body. He gently cleaned her with the bandanna, then rose and gathered her clothing. Lovingly he dressed her, carefully replacing the infrared beacon, then reached for his own clothes.

She said, "Thanks for...you know...protecting me."

He grimaced. "Not the most reliable method, but better than nothing. Next time I'll be prepared."

Next time. She tried not to let her uncertainty show, but he stared at her and said, "There will be a next time, Elizabeth. A lot of next times."

"I'm...confused."

"I know that, and I have no one to blame but myself." Half-dressed, he cradled her face in his palms. "You know, if I were the ruthless son of a bitch you think I am, I might've tried to get you pregnant. To make it harder for you to walk away from what we have."

"What do we have, Caleb?"

He started to say something and stopped. His thumb traced the line of her cheekbone and he dropped a featherlight kiss on her forehead. "Let me show you what we *can* have. Give me the chance to do that."

The temptation to fall into his arms, into his life, was nearly irresistible. She needed Caleb with a bone-deep intensity that frightened her.

But how could she know her heart at this point? Three weeks ago, with no warning, he'd brutally forced his presence on her. Since then he'd controlled every aspect of her life. She'd had contact with no one else and had been totally dependent on Caleb for all her needs.

Was her love for him genuine and freely given, or the warped attachment of a hostage to her captor? Only when she was free would she begin to sort out her mixed emotions. But the thought of getting away from Caleb left her feeling cold and hollow inside. Her acting career, her little apartment in Brooklyn—it all seemed like a previous incarnation.

She said, "Yesterday you asked me for time to figure things out."

"I figured them out. It didn't take that long." He smiled sadly.

"I know. And I'm glad. You don't know how much it means to me, to have your respect. And your faith. Now I'm asking you for the same thing, Caleb. Time. Time alone to sort things out."

He started to reach for her, then clenched his hand and dropped it. His eyes glowed with unswerving conviction. "All right, Elizabeth. Time. Alone. But I meant what I said. You belong to me now. You always will."

9

"DID HE HURT YOU, love?" Lugh slid his hand over the back of Elizabeth's neck. She fought down the urge to shake off the smooth, manicured fingers, so unlike Caleb's rough, callused ones.

"No. Not really. Just scared me is all."

He gently squeezed her neck, his green eyes glowing with warm concern, his British-accented voice silky. "Naturally, I reported your abduction, but the local constabulary leaves much to be desired, I'm sad to say."

Why do you look more smug than sad about that?

He continued, "We were frightfully worried about you, Beth. Some of the methods these deprogrammers use...well, I know of cases where young women have been...molested. And worse." He dipped his head and leveled an inquisitive stare from under thick, tawny eyebrows.

"No, um..." She swallowed hard. "Nothing like that happened."

He studied her expression for long, tense moments and finally said, "Good. I'm relieved to hear it."

The huge man standing behind Lugh stared fixedly at her. His dark, close-set eyes flicked down her body in insolent appraisal. Lugh noticed the direction of her gaze and turned briefly to glance behind him.

"Oh yes, there have been a few changes in your absence, love. After you were kidnapped, my closest advisers persuaded me to hire a bodyguard. Wayne here never leaves my side."

Wayne was tall and brawny. His dark hair was buzzed close to his craggy head, in sharp contrast to Lugh's thick blond braid. Wayne's smarmy stare made Elizabeth want to slink away and run straight back to Caleb.

She'd located Lugh in Avalon's ramshackle community room, originally the clubhouse of the summer camp that once occupied the property. Some sort of Halloween pep rally had just ended, and the members had filed out to scour the woods for branches to feed the bonfire to be lit that night. Enormous papier-mâché animal-head masks were arranged around the perimeter of the room, along with carved pumpkins that would later house lit candles.

Elizabeth said, "Do I still have my old room?"

"Absolutely. I knew you'd return to us, Beth. I felt it in the very fiber of my being. We're connected, you and I, in a very special way. There's a force drawing us together, a cosmic force. Do you feel it, too?"

"Uh, sure."

He placed his hands on her shoulders. His voice dropped suggestively. "I thought of you during the full moon."

When he remained silent, staring at her from under

those heavy eyebrows, she realized he was awaiting her response. She cleared her throat. "Yeah. Me, too."

He stroked her cheek. "Come to me tonight."

Her heart stopped. "Tonight? But—but there's no full moon tonight!"

His jaw flexed. "The bloody crescent moon will have to do. I've waited long enough. Come to me at midnight."

It wasn't a request.

"Yes, Lugh. I think I'll, uh, go to my room now, wash up a little."

"Fine. Run along."

She left the building with two pairs of eyes burning a hole in her back. The clock was ticking. If she didn't find anything worth reporting before midnight, she'd have to slip away empty-handed. For good. She'd never be able to return again, after cheating Lugh of the "bud of her innocence" twice.

KEEPING OUT OF SIGHT of the horde of commune members gathering branches was child's play for Caleb. He moved like a wraith. Now, perched in a tree, he slipped a pair of high-powered binoculars from his rucksack and trained them on the grounds around the main buildings. His patience was rewarded minutes later when Elizabeth came into view, walking between the clubhouse and the administration building. She glanced toward the woods, and her anxious gaze seemed to lock with his for one long, impossible moment.

"Don't do anything foolish, Elizabeth," he murmured, watching her disappear into a doorway. "Leave the fancy stuff to Rambo."

ELIZABETH'S ROOM had indeed remained undisturbed in her absence. She stood in the doorway, straining her ears for sounds of activity in the building. Nothing. Most everyone was in the woods, no doubt, getting ready for the celebration later.

Knowing she wouldn't get another opportunity like this, she silently slipped out of her room and down the carpeted hallway. She'd never before had a chance to snoop around Lugh's private suite. With the place empty, this was as good a time as any.

She let herself into his sitting room. Lugh seemed to favor expensive, ultramodern furnishings—leather, glass and plush imported carpets. She went through to the large bedroom. A king-size platform bed covered by a black satin comforter dominated the room. The rest of the furniture was black lacquer, and the walls were sheathed in mushroom-colored silk. It was a far cry from the members' squalid cabins.

The only other doors led to a sumptuous bathroom bigger than her bedroom, and a separate dressing room. Whatever nefarious activities were going on, they didn't seem to be going on here.

She'd just turned to leave when muted voices drifted through the suite from the closed door to the outer hallway. A man and a woman. The door started to creak open and Elizabeth panicked. The last thing she needed was to be caught poking around Lugh's bedroom.

She started toward the bathroom, but stopped short. If this was the cleaning crew, the bathroom was no place to hide. She couldn't crawl under the platform bed, with its solid pedestal. Frantically she glanced around the bedroom, and her gaze fell on the wardrobe. She raced to it, opened the mirrored doors and stepped inside, squeezing among Lugh's clothes. The voices suddenly became louder. She pulled the doors closed and found they didn't meet completely. The slim crack between them enabled her to peer into the room.

"...wants everyone out there at nine for the bonfire," the woman was saying as the two strolled into the bedroom.

"What about security around here?" the man asked.

"He'll have someone on duty. He figures one guy can hold down the fort during the party."

The two crossed to the wardrobe, and Elizabeth's heart nearly stopped. But they turned their backs and squatted at the fringed edge of the beautiful abstract area rug laid over the gleaming parquet floor. They rolled up the rug, revealing a large, stainless-steel panel set into the floor.

Elizabeth's eyes bulged as the man pulled a recessed handle to open a little door in the panel, exposing a keypad. She couldn't make out the tiny numbers, but as she watched him quickly key in four digits, she tried to burn the pattern into her memory—his forefinger made a check-mark shape on the keypad.

With a soft hissing sound, the steel trapdoor dropped several inches until it had cleared the wooden flooring, then slid open along the center seam. The space below was lit, but Elizabeth could see nothing except the first few carpeted steps.

Chattering about the coming celebration, the pair descended the stairs, disappearing into the secret basement. Only then did Elizabeth notice how airless the interior of the wardrobe had become. And hot. Her skin prickled, and sweat gathered between her breasts and under her arms. She could have sworn Lugh's clothes had multiplied in the past few moments, reaching for her, suffocating her.

Dare she leave while those two were still down there? No. She couldn't risk it. They could come up at any time. After an interminable few minutes, they re-emerged, the woman carrying a fat brown envelope. The man pushed a button on the exposed edge of the trapdoor, which silently slid closed. They rolled the rug back into place and strolled out of the suite.

Elizabeth crept from her hiding place. The secret cellar had to be the location of whatever dirty business Lugh was up to—whatever had gotten David and Tessa killed. Elation warred with raw fear. She wanted nothing more than to toss aside the rug under her feet and explore Lugh's underground activities. But now wasn't the time. Even if the two lackeys she'd just seen didn't return, someone else might come upon her—perhaps Lugh himself.

No, she'd wait until nine o'clock, when everyone would be at the bonfire. They'd said only one guard would be on duty. As she carefully made her way out of the suite and the building, she thought about the promise she'd made to Caleb. She'd sworn to do nothing more than look around for likely locations, and wait for him to join her at ten o'clock so he could do the actual investigating—the breaking and entering.

That plan made sense, yet how could she pass up the opportunity to do a little exploring on her own when the place was practically deserted? Afterward she'd meet Caleb as scheduled and they'd go directly to the police with whatever she uncovered.

As she casually strolled outside to join the rest of the commune in a search for branches, she envisioned the gleam of pride that would light Caleb's eyes when she dropped the evidence in his lap. A secret half smile curved her mouth.

WHAT THE HELL was she doing? Caleb held the night-vision goggles to his eyes. From his position near the edge of the woods he had a good view of the main buildings of the compound. It was a little after nine and he'd just done recon deep in the woods to the east, where the commune members had constructed a massive bonfire in a clearing.

Most of them wore white robes and huge masks of animals that covered their entire heads. A motley ensemble played discordant music on guitars, tambourines and recorders, while others danced around the bonfire with their jack-o'-lanterns, laughing and singing, obviously enjoying this rare respite from their labors.

As he peered through the goggles, night became green-tinted day. He watched a lone figure skirt around the cabins toward the administration building. From high on the torso came the steady little light—the infrared beacon visible only to him—that told him he was watching the woman he loved. But what was she doing? Why wasn't she with the others? Hadn't she had plenty of time earlier to snoop around the building?

Damn. What if Lugh came looking for her?

Caleb growled, "Get back to the wingding, Mata Hari. Don't start getting cute on me now."

Why had he ever agreed to let her do this? He should have listened to his instincts—hog-tied her if that's what it took—and made this a solo mission. He'd never forgive himself if she got hurt.

"I'M RELIEVING YOU," Elizabeth said.

The guard eyed her suspiciously from his post just inside the administration building. He was a freckle-faced redhead in his early twenties. She didn't remember him; he must have joined recently.

He said, "I'm here all night, is what they told me. Who're you, anyway?"

"Beth Russell. I just got back—"

"Hey, I heard of you! Aren't you that girl that was snatched a few weeks ago?"

"Yeah, that's right. My family hired a deprogrammer."

"Wow. Was it, like, as bad as they say?"

"I can't begin to describe it."

"So how'd you get away?"

"I pretended I was some kind of helpless, wimpy female. When he let down his guard I overpowered him and escaped. Lugh was so impressed, he put me on the security force. Sure beats scrubbing the john." She jerked her head toward the party. "Go on. I can handle things here."

The guard puffed his cheeks with the effort of cogitation. "I don't know...I wanna join the fun, but they told me I gotta stay here."

Elizabeth extracted her semiautomatic from her jacket and showed it to him. "Lugh gave me this and said to tell you to find a costume and enjoy the rest of the party." Only the security force were armed.

He relaxed. "Cool. I'm outta here. See ya around."

The instant he left, she hurried to Lugh's quarters, rolled up the rug over the trapdoor and exposed the keypad. She wiped her sweaty palms on her jacket and concentrated on envisioning the pattern she'd seen the man key in earlier. Her finger hovered over the pad and then she tapped the four numbers.

The steel trapdoor dropped and slid open with a hiss. Elizabeth said a silent *yes!* She took a deep breath and descended the carpeted steps into a large, bright room. Whatever she expected to see, it wasn't this: a clean, well-equipped office, chock-full of the latest in high-tech equipment.

She saw a couple of computers, complete with a top-of-the-line color laser printer. Nearby sat something that looked like a desktop photocopier. Closer inspection revealed it to be a scanner, used to transfer photographs or printed material directly into a computer. In the corner sat a large photocopier. She perused the controls and realized it was a color copier. A massive, well-lit worktable occupied one wall.

She did a slow three-sixty, staring at these pricey gizmos. Was she totally off base in her suspicions? Could Lugh be hiding all this stuff away just to keep the grubby hands of the commune members off it?

Along one wall, in the midst of this high-tech haven, were a clothes washer and dryer. She frowned. *What's wrong with this picture?* She opened the lid of the washer. Empty. She was about to close it when something caught her eye. She reached in and peeled a damp piece of paper off the inside of the washer tub.

And stood staring at a twenty-dollar bill.

Realization struck in a sickening rush. Stunned, she gaped at her surroundings with a fresh eye.

Lugh was a counterfeiter!

She turned the bill over in her hand. It looked perfect. She'd heard that fake bills were often laundered prior to circulation to give them a worn look.

Was this one damp faux twenty enough evidence to interest the police? Somehow she doubted it. She had to do better than that, but she'd been down there too long already. It wouldn't be long before Lugh discovered the guard had deserted his post. She hoped to be on the other side of the compound by then.

She scurried around the room yanking open drawers and cabinets, searching frantically. On the worktable lay an open box labeled Rice Paper. She fingered a sheet. It had the feel of crisp new money. She lifted the top of a small cardboard box near it—and sucked in a sharp breath. Stacked inside were bundles of twenties, each secured with a blue rubber band over a strip of yellow paper.

She grabbed a bundle and tucked it in her jacket pocket next to her gun. At the foot of the stairs she paused and listened intently. When silence greeted her, she let out the breath she'd been holding and crept back up to Lugh's bedroom. She pushed the button that closed the trapdoor and replaced the rug.

Within seconds she was outside, trying to keep from running as she crossed the grounds toward the distant garage where she was to meet Caleb. She breathed a sigh of relief.

"Beth! Wherever are you going, love?"

Lugh's voice slammed into her from out of the gloom. She froze, deafened by her own pulse, and squinted into a flashlight beam now trained on her face.

Lugh chided, "Wayne, be nice...."

The light beam slowly descended, lingering on her chest, which rose and fell rapidly as she struggled for composure. Her jacket still lay open and she imagined they could see her heart hammering her rib cage.

The flashlight clicked off, and now she could just make out the moonlit forms of the two men. Lugh wore a white robe and a papier-mâché raven-head mask. She recalled that ravens were associated with the Celtic god Lugh. Wayne towered over his boss. He, too, was clad in a white robe, along with a hideous bear-head mask, complete with fangs. The masks enclosed their entire heads.

Wayne grunted. A man of few words.

Lugh translated. "Wayne wants to know why you're dashing into the woods, Beth. I must say, such behavior is...curious." The raven head turned to peer in the direction she was headed—away from the commune's buildings, away from the bonfire. He turned back and silently awaited an explanation.

She swallowed a knot of terror and faced him squarely. "I...got kind of disoriented, I guess. I thought everyone was..." She shrugged and nodded toward the inky woods.

Silence reigned for a heart-stopping few moments. Lugh sighed resignedly. He gestured toward her. "Wayne..."

The huge man handed the flashlight to Lugh and came at her. She tried not to cringe as his meaty hands patted her down and reached into her jacket pocket.

When he grunted again, it sounded like "Gotcha!"

10

CALEB'S FINGERS tightened painfully on the night-vision goggles when he saw the bodyguard put his hands on Elizabeth. Wayne pulled something out of her pocket—her gun, he assumed—and Lugh reacted. Caleb knew it was Lugh under that ridiculous raven mask; he'd been keeping track of the commune leader for hours.

Elizabeth's hand fluttered to her chest. The steady light signal started to blink.

"No kidding," Caleb growled. "What the hell have you done, Elizabeth?"

As if she heard him, she threw a panicked glance in his direction before the bodyguard roughly hauled her back toward the administration building.

"I'm coming for you, sweetheart." He lowered the goggles. "Just hang in there."

WAYNE SHOVED ELIZABETH onto a silk-upholstered armchair in Lugh's bedroom. She looked into his mean dark eyes through the small holes in the gigantic bear-head mask he still wore, probably to scare her spitless on some visceral level.

It was working.

Lugh, however, pulled off his mask and set it aside.

He smoothed a few errant strands of blond hair off his face. She'd never seen him look so frigidly remote. This wasn't the same man who'd waxed poetic a few hours ago about a "cosmic force" drawing them together. This man was capable of anything.

Wayne had pulled a hefty semiautomatic out of his robe the instant they entered the building. Now Lugh produced one as well, and trained it on her even as he spoke to his bodyguard.

"Who's supposed to be watching the building tonight?"

The bear grunted. She thought it sounded like "Paul," though it could have been "Saul" or even "Y'all."

"Find him." The rest went unsaid.

She didn't envy the hapless guard.

Wayne left and Lugh came to stand over her. He held the bundle of twenties, with its distinctive yellow-and-blue banding. It would be preposterous for her to try to claim she'd gotten it anywhere but from the secret chamber directly below them.

"So." He tapped the bundle against her cheek. "Is this what you were after all along, love, or did you just get nosy? And greedy?"

Caleb, did you see the signal? Do you know I need you?

It was still a good twenty minutes or so till ten o'clock, when she was supposed to meet him. If he hadn't noticed the blinking signal, he wouldn't figure out something was wrong till then. She didn't want to think about what this man and his taciturn bodyguard could do to her in twenty minutes.

He closed in, till his white robe brushed her trembling knees. He pressed the barrel of the weapon against her temple, his voice far too soft and silky for comfort. "When I ask a question, Beth, I expect an immediate answer. Is that understood?"

She stared up at him defiantly.

"You didn't join Avalon for the wholesome country air, did you, love." He'd begun figuring it out. "And here I thought I'd covered all my tracks. Well, it only goes to show—one can't be too careful. Tell me, are you really a virgin?"

He tossed the bills onto his bed and reached for her breast. She recoiled and shoved his hand away. Even more than sheer revulsion at his touch, she was terrified of him finding the little Firefly. If he suspected she had an accomplice, both she and Caleb would be in even greater danger.

He chuckled. "Perhaps so. Well, not to worry, love. You shan't be burdened by your sexual inexperience for long. I'll see to that." His grin was malignant. "And so will Wayne. And afterward...well, let's just say that afterward you won't be burdened by anything ever again."

"Are you going to hang me, like you did David?"

His eyes slowly widened. "Well. Surprise surprise. How do you know David?"

She didn't dare sneak a peek at her watch. "Or are you going to have me strangled and dumped in the woods like Tessa?"

His face twisted in an ugly scowl. "Tessa turned on me. They both did. And they paid the price."

Wayne reentered the room, still in full regalia—robe, mask, gun. Keeping his own gun pressed to her temple, Lugh said, "That was fast. Did you take care of Raoul?"

The bear grunted.

Lugh smiled appreciatively at his bodyguard. "Well, at least I can count on someone. I was just explaining to the young lady the price of betrayal. Now, let's see, Beth...you could've learned about Tessa on the news, but my guess is you actually *knew* David Trent. Am I right?" He caressed her temple with the gun barrel. "Hmm?"

She trembled with fear and rage. "Go to hell."

Wayne grunted with uncharacteristic eloquence, and Lugh grinned as he translated, "There isn't much doubt of that, now is there?"

Déjà vu. That's just how Caleb had answered the same barb that afternoon. She glanced at the bodyguard. He was staring intently at her. She shivered, realizing Lugh intended to share her with him. Would he keep the mask on?

Lugh said, "David Trent never mentioned a Beth. How do you know him?"

Caleb, please hurry! "He was a friend."

"Does he have any more friends foolish enough to risk their lives playing junior detective?" Lugh moved the gun downward. Her throat constricted as she felt the barrel tickle her neck. He said, "What about the girl he called the day he died. Lizzie."

He must have seen it in her eyes. He gave a startled

laugh, then said, "Ah, of course. Lizzie. Beth. Elizabeth."

"Took you long enough to figure it out."

His tone was one of mock admiration. "Such spirit, in the face of such trying circumstances. I must say, you don't have much in common with your dear departed friend. David was weak. And so wonderfully malleable."

"Not so malleable if you had to kill him to protect your operation."

Wayne had taken up a position near them, gun at the ready, his stance tense as if he expected her to leap up at any moment and make a run for it.

Lugh's gun barrel dug into her neck. "He brought it on himself. When Tessa Montgomery suffered a pang of conscience and threatened to expose my enterprise, we were forced to exercise damage control."

"Why don't you just call it murder?"

He tipped his head, conceding the point. "Unfortunately, your David witnessed her demise and became quite agitated. He 'freaked out,' to put it in the vernacular. Well, he was so unstable, naturally I had him watched. He turned out to be more clever than we gave him credit for. Managed to slip away from my people long enough to find a phone. Of course, I'd had the foresight to have listening devices installed. One cannot be too careful."

Elizabeth was sickened with the realization that it was David's desperate phone call to her that had gotten him killed. They'd hanged him and made it look like suicide.

Lugh continued, "David was exceedingly useful to me while he cooperated. A brilliant graphic artist. Which is why I targeted him in the first place, of course. He was ambivalent about joining Avalon, concerned about his family's reaction—there's some straight-arrow brother somewhere." He gave a smug grin. "As if I'd let a prize like him slip through my fingers."

She squeezed the arms of her chair, thinking of insecure David in the clutches of this master manipulator. "No doubt you exploited his insecurities to make him join the commune and take part in the counterfeiting."

Lugh smirked. "I offered the boy *counseling*, love. I listened to his troubles. Such a needy young man, so...lost."

"So loaded."

"That, too. David enriched us in so very many ways. But make no mistake, his artistic talent was as valuable to me as his net worth. He was a welcome addition to my private staff. The inner sanctum."

"Your counterfeiters, you mean. That's what Avalon's really about, only most of the members are oblivious."

He shrugged. "I needed a front for my little business. The Avalon Collective was a stroke of genius, if I do say so. We're an isolated, autonomous community, and the occasional well-placed campaign contribution helps keep the local authorities from sniffing around. To the outside world we look like a bunch of flower-child throwbacks. I simply drew on my natural leadership ability. People look up to me. They always have."

"Yeah, it must really stroke your ego to have all these losers looking to you for life's answers...all those confused and trusting women falling at your feet."

"It's a tough job, but..." He shrugged.

She tried to avoid looking at Wayne, who stared intently at her. Lugh's gun dug into her throat, but she concentrated on keeping him talking. Buying time. "What do you do with all that counterfeit money?"

"My connections with certain, shall we say, pharmaceutical entrepreneurs have proven immensely profitable."

"You're involved in the drug trade?"

"Such a crass way to put it, but accurate enough, I suppose. My associates find the fake bills quite useful in swindling *their* associates, the South American drug cartels."

"And if you occasionally have to murder someone to keep him quiet, well, hell, that's just part of the cost of doing business, right?"

There was a long pause before Lugh said, "David told me all about you, you know. Beautiful Lizzie, so pure, so unattainable."

She squeezed her eyes shut.

"The silly boy practically deified you. You know, you'd have been wiser to spread your pretty legs for him—chip away a little of the mystery, the saintly aura in which he'd cloaked you. Oh yes, love, he shared all the tiresome details with me. How he carried a torch for you all those years, without a scrap of encouragement on your part. How shocked and dismayed you were when he finally confessed his love for you. Why, you devastated the poor lad."

She glared at him, his image wavering before her burning eyes. "David might've had his problems, but he had integrity. He was a good person."

He affected a wounded air. "Unlike *moi?*"

"You're not even in the same species, Graham."

"The name is Lugh."

She studied him, as if contemplating that. "Come to think of it, Lugh does fit you better. Isn't that what you British call the john? The loo?"

She watched his scowl twist into a rictus of hatred, and tensed as his free arm swung back to strike her.

She hadn't even seen Wayne move, yet suddenly there he was, gripping his boss's wrist.

Lugh blinked up at his bodyguard in bemusement and wrenched his arm free. He shoved his gun harder against her throat. "Don't fret, Wayne. I won't mess her up too much before you get a crack at her."

Wayne squatted in front of Elizabeth and peered at her from behind his bear-head mask. Reflexively she turned away, wishing she were stronger, braver. She felt his callused fingers on her jaw, brutally forcing her to face him.

The fearsome mask was inches from her. Her stomach had turned to jelly, but she put steel in her spine and made herself look at him.

Her heart stopped and she choked back a strangled gasp. Silver gray eyes stared back at her from the mask's eyeholes.

Caleb's eyes!

Lugh said, "She's a pretty little thing, no? A pity really." Obviously referring to her impending death.

Caleb grunted, Wayne-style. Without moving his head, he directed his gaze pointedly to the gun barrel pressed to her throat. She got the message: overpowering Lugh right now would be too risky. She could end up dead.

With her eyes she sent a silent message. *I'll take my cues from you. But do something!*

"Well?" Lugh asked, obviously amused by the big man's intense scrutiny of Elizabeth. "Does she pass muster?"

Caleb grunted in the affirmative and stood up.

Lugh caressed her cheek with his free hand. "It's party time, love. Come now. Don't be shy."

He pulled her up out of the chair. Reflexively she cringed away from him, and he pressed the gun barrel into her neck till she winced in pain. She heard her own whimper and bit her lip to keep from pleading with him.

Lugh said, "Don't fight me, Beth. If you do, I'll be forced to make this exceedingly unpleasant for you. As entertaining as that prospect is, I *did* promise Wayne there'd be something left over for him."

Caleb stood a few feet away, his stance tense, his own gun at the ready. She hazarded a glance at him and saw the mask nod. Ever so slightly. *Go along with him—for the moment.* She squeezed her eyes shut and swallowed hard. And forced herself to relax slightly.

Lugh turned to Caleb. "Feel free to stay and watch if you'd like, Wayne."

Caleb nodded.

Lugh chuckled. "Well. Still waters run deep. And you'll return the favor, of course, dear boy. I wouldn't want to miss that—sort of an X-rated Beauty and the Beast, I should think. Now, Beth..." He fingered the lapel of her jacket. "Let's get these clothes off you and see what we have, hmm?"

"Umm..." She licked her dry lips and angled her eyes to the gun at her throat. "It would be easier if you could just move that."

"No. Now, give us a good show, love. Make me want to keep you around for a while."

As he spoke, he slowly trailed the tip of the gun barrel down her throat and chest, into the V of her open shirt collar. His green eyes were mean and taunting as the barrel slid between her breasts. She held her breath, praying he wouldn't find—

Click.

She jerked as steel met the hard plastic casing of the Firefly. Lugh froze for a second, his frigid gaze boring into her. He said to Caleb, "You should've patted her down a tad more thoroughly. Now, what could this be? A little snubby, perhaps?"

When he thrust his fingers into her cleavage, she saw Caleb stiffen. His knuckles gleamed white on the grip of his gun.

Lugh lifted out the small electronic device. He turned it in his hand, examining it with interest. And smiled. "Ah. Yes. I've come across this doodah in the spy shops. A cunning little device, really. Have you ever seen one of these, Wayne?" He handed the Firefly to Caleb, who studied it with a perplexed grunt. "It's an infrared marking beacon. Which means, of course—" his expression chilled Elizabeth to her bones "—that the young lady has an accomplice."

He gripped her arm hard. "Who?" When she said nothing he twisted her arm behind her back. It hurt like hell and she couldn't suppress a groan. "You *will* tell me. Make it easy on yourself."

When she remained mute, he said, "Wayne, get a couple of the others to fan out and search the grounds for interlopers. *Discreetly*, of course."

The pain in her shoulder was blinding. Tears streamed down Elizabeth's face and she willed herself not to pass out.

Lugh tapped her temple with the gun. "Have you ever had a dislocated shoulder, Beth? You're about to find out what it feels like. Then I'll begin breaking your ribs, one by one," he added pleasantly. "After that, well, I can be very imaginative. Of course, that sort of activity can be like eating potato crisps. Once you get started, it's a devil to stop. As I said, you *will* tell me what I want to know." He pulled hard on her arm and she screamed. "Sooner or later."

Suddenly he noticed Caleb was still there. The gun swung away from her as Lugh gesticulated with it. "What are you waiting for, Wayne?"

"That," Caleb said, and squeezed off a shot.

Lugh shrieked and grabbed his hand as his gun went flying. Elizabeth leaped away from him and threw herself at his weapon. Rolling into a crouch, she drew a bead on the commune leader, wordlessly daring him to make a move. Spears of pain shot down her arm, but she held the gun steady.

Caleb's voice was filled with admiration. "We could've used you in the Delta Force, sweetheart."

Lugh's incredulous, pain-filled gaze darted from one to the other. "Bloody hell," he whispered. "She's found herself a bloody commando."

Caleb drew Elizabeth to his side. She said, "That gunshot's going to bring 'em running, Caleb. I bet they heard it at the bonfire."

"I know. Get something for his hand."

Lugh's wound was spurting blood onto the abstract carpet under his feet. Crimson spatters decorated his white robe.

As Elizabeth pocketed her gun and grabbed a towel from the bathroom, Caleb said, "We're all going to walk out of here together. You've suffered an unfortunate accident, Graham. Your bodyguard and your devoted follower—" he nodded toward Elizabeth as she returned and began wrapping the injured hand "—are taking you to the emergency room." He nudged Lugh's nose with his gun. "That's the story, and if you want to live, you'll stick to it."

"Bravo, Mr. Schwarzenegger," Lugh sneered. "I'm positively quaking in my boots. Pardon me for not applauding. Ow!"

Elizabeth had tightened the makeshift bandage with a touch more enthusiasm than was strictly required.

"You don't think I'd kill you?" Caleb asked with chilling calm.

Lugh's spontaneous bark of laughter made her want to shoot his other hand. Still, she had to admire his aplomb. Cradling his injury, he said, "I may be going out on a limb here, but I'd wager that summary executions of wounded, unarmed men are not quite the thing among you Delta blokes."

Elizabeth kept a close eye on Caleb's tense trigger finger, wondering if Lugh's smirking arrogance was about to earn him a third nostril. Suddenly they heard shouts and running feet entering the building. Triumph glittered in the commune leader's eyes.

Caleb tapped Lugh's nose with the barrel of his gun. "Oh, did I happen to mention? David Trent was my baby brother."

As the words sank in, Lugh's face sagged and lost all color. He mouthed what looked like *bloody hell*.

Caleb loosened the top of his robe and slipped the semiautomatic into his shoulder holster, where it would be instantly accessible. He adjusted his mask.

Three men and a woman, all armed, stormed into the room. The guy in charge—long hair, shaggy beard, trailer-hitch bald spot—demanded, "What was that shot?" His eyes zeroed in on Lugh's hand and the bloodstained towel.

Elizabeth said, "Lugh's gun accidentally went off. We're taking him to the emergency room." She and Caleb each took an arm and started pulling him toward the door.

The storm troopers exchanged uneasy glances. Baldy moved to block the exit. "Lugh...?"

She said, "Can't you see he's in shock? Move, dammit!" She patted Lugh's injured hand consolingly—ending with a good hard squeeze.

Lugh jumped. "Move, you bloody fool!"

Baldy shuffled out of the way. He turned to the female guard. "Bring the Bimmer around." As she ran out of the building, he unhooked a walkie-talkie from his belt and instructed the guards at the compound entrance to open the gates. Elizabeth and Caleb hauled Lugh down the corridor and out into the chilly night. Distant sounds of music and laughter told her the revelers were still going at it.

A minute later Lugh's BMW pulled up and the female guard hopped out, leaving the motor running. Caleb grunted at Elizabeth, indicating she should drive.

Baldy said, "Hey, Wayne. Better lose the mask before you get to the hospital." Caleb ignored him and reached for the back door handle.

All heads turned at what sounded like the bellow of a wounded animal, fast approaching from around the building.

"Get in!" Caleb hollered, yanking open the driver's door and shoving Elizabeth into the car.

The running figure turned into a battered-looking Wayne, loping toward them with surprising speed for a man his size. Snarling with rage, he wrenched a gun from one of the guards as they stood gaping from him to the big masked, robed man now throwing open the BMW's back door and hurling their leader inside.

Caleb ducked and returned fire as Wayne's first shot pinged off the car. The bodyguard jerked and tottered a bit with a chest wound that would have dropped a rhino. Caleb leaped into the car just as Wayne squeezed off a few more rounds.

Elizabeth knew immediately that Caleb had been hit. She screamed his name.

"*Drive!*" he yelled. "*Go go go go!*" She stomped on the accelerator as he pulled the door closed and tugged off the mask.

The guards finally grasped the situation enough to begin firing at the retreating car, but the bullets failed to penetrate the vehicle's body or the rear windshield. She glanced into the rearview mirror. Baldy was yammering into his walkie-talkie, probably alerting the guards at the entrance.

"You!" Caleb barked at Lugh. "Don't move a goddamn hair."

Elizabeth raced along the twisty-turny road toward the gate, trying to keep control of the wheel with sweat-slick hands. "Caleb, where are you hit?"

"Leg," he rasped. "And my side."

"Oh God." Silently she mouthed a string of profanities. She glanced over her shoulder to see crimson stains spreading fast on his white robe and the car's buttery leather upholstery.

He held his gun to Lugh's ribs. "Keep your eyes on the road!" he barked at her.

Her pulse thundered in her ears. "How bad is it?"

"Just drive."

Now she mouthed a string of prayers.

The compound's entrance came into view, illuminated by floodlights. As they sped toward it, the motorized gate slid closed. Two guards dashed out of the gatehouse, crouched and began firing on the car. She yelped and ducked her head, skidding to a stop, but the bullets merely thunked into the windshield, embedding themselves in the thick plastic.

Caleb's eyebrows rose. "This kind of custom armoring must've set you back a fortune in phony-baloney bucks, Graham. Very nice."

"Thank you," Lugh said through gritted teeth.

"Tires reinforced, too?"

"Naturally."

The guards stopped firing as it became clear the vehicle was impregnable. A van came tearing up behind them. The storm troopers tumbled out and took up offensive positions. The BMW was blocked in.

Caleb seized Lugh in a headlock and pressed the gun to his temple, quivering with pain and blood loss. Sweat beaded on his ashen face. Nevertheless, he kept a firm grip on the commune leader, making sure the guards had a good view.

"Tell them to open the gate."

Lugh's voice was a hoarse whisper. "Open the gate."

"Louder!"

"Open the gate! Open the bloody gate!" Lugh screeched, choking on terror and impotent rage. His eyes bulged in their sockets.

The guards eyed each other and, as one, looked behind the BMW to where Baldy had his assault rifle trained on the car. Glaring malevolently, he shook his head no.

Caleb jerked Lugh around to face the obstinate headman. He said, "So, Graham. Tell me how it went with David. Did my brother beg for mercy? Did you stay to watch? I know you like to watch."

"Open the gate, you idiots! *Open it!*"

With a venomous curse Baldy lowered his rifle and signaled to the guards. The gate slid open and Elizabeth gunned it. As they raced toward the highway, the assault rifle spat a few last harmless rounds.

11

"UPS WILL PICK THESE UP tomorrow." Elizabeth kept her eyes on the carton she was sealing with packing tape.

She walked to the lowboy dresser and laid the tape dispenser on the gleaming wood, then glanced up and saw Caleb's reflection in the mirror. He stood in the doorway of her bedroom, leaning on the frame. Watching her. His face was rigid.

She met his eyes in the mirror. "Are you in pain?"

"No."

The wounds he'd incurred during their flight from Avalon two weeks ago were healing well. She was amazed by his resilience. He still walked with a limp but no longer needed a cane. Or her.

She'd never forget her panic and anguish after the emergency-room personnel had rushed Caleb into surgery. Hour after hour she'd waited for word of his condition. When they'd asked what her relationship was to the patient, it took her a long moment to come up with "friend."

Prisoner. Lover. Comrade-in-arms. Friend. She hadn't been able to sort it out then, and she was no closer to doing so now.

During his stay in the hospital and his convalescence afterward, she'd willingly stuck by him, taking care of him, nursing him back to health. She wouldn't have trusted that job to anyone else.

They hadn't made love again. Her choice. He'd made overtures, of course, even when he was obviously still too weak. She'd sensed his desperate urgency, his need to bind her to himself in this most elemental way. The truth was, she felt the same urgency, but refused to succumb to it. She needed to distance herself from him, to try to get a handle on what they truly meant to each other.

Their relationship, if she could call it that, consisted of pure emotion. Peaks and valleys of passion without form or substance. A bizarre association forged of lies and coercion, and nurtured in the bubble of their insulated existence.

Could such a relationship survive the real world? Would it evolve and grow? Or would it dry up and blow away in the unforgiving light of day? And could she bear it if it did?

She'd worked hard for years, overcome tremendous odds to carve out a niche for herself in that real world. Now she was consumed with the need to rediscover that niche, to shore up her career and the independence she'd taken for granted until a few short weeks ago. To prove to herself she was still master of her life.

She turned and faced him. "I'll call a taxi to take me to the airport."

He didn't move, but his eyes did. They caressed her features. "Let me come see you."

"No." They'd been through this.

"When will you contact me?" he asked. "How long will it take for you to realize we belong together?" When she remained silent, he said, "Will I ever see you again?"

She swallowed hard. *Don't ask me that,* she silently pleaded, afraid she knew the answer. "You've convinced yourself that I'm abandoning you. You know that's not the way it is."

His mirthless chuckle said he knew no such thing.

She took a deep breath. "The usual rules don't apply to us. All bets were off the day I found myself trussed up and gagged and lying helpless and terrified in the back of your Land Rover. The day you decided to play God with my life."

His spontaneous, unguarded expression tore at her resolve. Just for an instant he looked almost vulnerable. In the sudden, eerie stillness he stared at her, and she met his intense silver gaze unflinchingly, surprised by the depth of anger still simmering deep inside. Her lingering resentment was another reason she had to leave him, something else to work through.

She knew he deeply regretted his actions. He claimed to love her. He'd told her so many times during the last two weeks, when he'd tried to convince her to stay, to build on whatever it was they had. Just as she feared that her feelings for Caleb were an unhealthy psychological dependence on her captor, she had to wonder how great a role guilt played in his declarations of love.

He said, "I told you I'd make it up to you, but I can't

do that if you run away from me, dammit! I'm just getting back on my feet. Give me a chance to—"

"You no longer need me."

"Like hell."

"You know what I mean. You can take care of yourself now. You knew I'd be leaving as soon as you were strong enough."

He smiled sadly. "I guess I thought you'd changed your mind. It was...nice between us these last couple of weeks. Sweet."

She struggled to ignore his wistful tone. It *had* been sweet between them, once Caleb was out of danger. She'd gotten a brief taste of what life could be like for them, coexisting as equals.

Or was she just fooling herself? Their roles had reversed during Caleb's convalescence, putting her in a position of power. He'd been dependent on her for his needs, just as she'd once been dependent on him. She reminded herself that, the last two placid weeks notwithstanding, this man was, after all, her spike-chomping commando. He'd been hurt before—far worse than this. She had little doubt that once he was completely recovered, he'd be his old overbearing self. Men like this didn't miraculously transform into Alan Alda.

Elizabeth started to move past him through the doorway. Neither looked at the other, even when his hand snaked out to bar the way. She didn't push past him. She could have, but she didn't. The truth was, she craved this. The drugging scent of him, the possessive heat of his touch.

His arm tightened around her waist, pulling her to his side. He turned his head and nuzzled her hair, and she closed her eyes and slumped against him.

In a few short hours she'd be back home in Brooklyn, calling her agent and slipping into her old routine. She'd allow herself this one last bittersweet moment.

He lifted her hair and pressed his lips to the sensitive curve between neck and shoulder. And again, a bare inch away, and yet again. His kisses were soft, unhurried, as if he was savoring the taste of her. The warm imprint of his lips lingered on her skin. She melted into him, boneless, her head dropping.

She didn't realize she'd said his name until he responded, "Hmm?"

"I don't want to leave," she confessed, the words barely audible.

His lips found the delicate bumps of her vertebrae. Shivering sparks raced down her spine, branching into a ghostly net of sensations linking her most intimate places.

His breath whispered over her neck when he responded at last. "I know you don't."

But I know you have to. She heard the unspoken words.

"I hate this," she said, tears leaking from the corners of her closed eyes. "God, I hate this."

He curled her into him, her back to his front, his long arms banded around her. She clung to his arms and blinked away the tears, drawing deep, shuddering breaths to keep the sobs at bay.

He dipped his head to whisper in her ear, "Be good to yourself, Elizabeth. Do it for me."

12

FROM HIS CONCEALED location deep in the shadows, Caleb watched the woman he loved slide into another man's arms.

Elizabeth clutched Tony's tuxedo jacket and stared adoringly into his eyes, her own misted with passion. Her magnificent body was sheathed in a clingy, red sequined evening gown. Backless. Slit to the thigh. Illegal cleavage. Light-years from his denim-and-flannel captive.

She purred, "I feel like I've known you forever, Tony. Can it only be...eleven days?"

"Twelve." Tony chuckled, stroking her bare back. "But who's counting?"

Caleb drew a slow, deep breath and forced his jaw to unclench. He hadn't seen her in over three months. Not since she'd packed up her meager belongings and run back to the city. Away from him.

Now, watching her with Tony, Caleb was forced to admit his beautiful Elizabeth hadn't spent the last three months pining for him. No, the lady had kept herself very busy indeed, while he'd done his damnedest to resume his life, throwing himself into his security-consulting business and maintenance of the estate. But each day without her brought more cruel reminders of the warm, vital woman who'd shared his life for one precious month....

Precious? He grimaced. To him, maybe. He knew that to Elizabeth, that interlude in her life had been frustrating and humiliating at best. Downright terrifying at times. Hadn't he made sure of that? No doubt she wanted nothing more than to forget the nightmare he'd subjected her to.

To forget him.

But try as he might, he couldn't forget her. His dreams were filled with the feel of her, the scent of her. She was burned into his soul, a part of him.

He recalled their conversation in Avalon's garage, after they'd made love. Hadn't he warned her then that if she left, he'd find her, that she belonged to him now? As far as he was concerned, three months was more than enough time for her to decide she needed him. So here he was, coming after her once again—tracking and bagging his elusive quarry.

This time for keeps.

He watched tall, handsome Tony thread his fingers through her long, glossy brown hair and tip her head back. Saw the stark yearning in his eyes as he lowered his lips to hers.

Caleb crushed the play program in his fist. The woman sitting in front of him shot a glare over her shoulder. He cleared his throat and shifted on the hard wooden bench. Onstage, Elizabeth's ersatz lover swept her into a toe-curling clinch of a kiss as darkness descended, to thunderous applause.

Seconds later, the stage lights snapped on, and she

and the other players took their bows. Caleb wondered how she'd react if she knew he was in the audience. Would the knowledge thrill her—or would that dazzling smile falter? Damn, his palms were clammy. He felt like he was about to face a few dozen heavily armed terrorists.

A stagehand brought out an enormous bouquet of pink roses, which Tony presented to Elizabeth to mark this, the final performance of *Stranger Things*, a contemporary romantic comedy by an unknown Neil Simon wannabe. The director appeared onstage, to a roaring standing ovation. Caleb unfolded himself from the butt-numbing bench and joined in the accolades.

At last the stage emptied and the houselights went up. He made his way down the bleacher-style seats that adjoined the small proscenium stage. The auditorium was so cozy that during the barroom brawl in Act Two the front-row patrons had been forced to pull in their feet to avoid becoming part of the action.

This storefront walk-up theater forty blocks north of Times Square had been billed as "off-Broadway." Caleb decided a few extra "offs" might be more accurate. Still, the production had been surprisingly professional, and Elizabeth had, of course, been outstanding in the lead role.

Now, if only he could cast her as his own leading lady, he'd consider his mission a success.

He shuffled out of the cramped auditorium with the fifty or so other playgoers and managed to locate his shearling jacket in the cluttered coatroom. He approached the young woman who'd sold him his ticket. "I'm a friend of Elizabeth Lancaster's. Where can I find her?"

She pointed down a long corridor. "The women's dressing room. She'll be out in a few minutes."

He positioned himself behind a corner where he could unobtrusively observe the door to the dressing room. He waited as actors and actresses drifted by on their way out. Ten minutes passed...fifteen. He thought of her peeling off that slinky red thing, wriggling out of it...

Muttering under his breath, he fastened his long jacket over the subversive part of him that screamed, *To hell with time and distance and sorting things out— grab her by the hair and drag her back to the cave, dammit! Now!*

His reflexes kicked into high gear when he spied her coming out of the dressing room, wearing a puffy, waist-length ski jacket over a long, swingy skirt and scuffed cowboy boots. He grinned. No slave to fashion, his Elizabeth.

No sooner had she entered the corridor, slinging a large purse over her shoulder, than someone else who'd apparently been waiting for her stepped forward. This guy was short, slim, self-possessed. She appeared leery at first—had she encountered her share of stage-door Johnnies?—but was soon all smiles. Her eyes glowed and a blush stained her cheeks. They scooted into an out-of-the-way corner to continue their conversation.

Caleb's eyes narrowed. Just how busy had she been these last three months?

After watching them chat for several minutes, he could stand it no longer. Abandoning his covert observation post, he strolled down the corridor within plain view of Elizabeth. She never glanced at him; all her attention was on her new pal and their animated conversation. She beamed at Slim with an expression that could only be called dreamy. Caleb couldn't decide what he wanted to do more—kiss that goofy look off her face or feed the guy to a wood chipper. Feetfirst.

As Caleb stepped up to the pair, Slim presented her with a business card, which she handled as if it were the Shroud of Turin. "So I'll be in touch," he said. "We'll set something up for next week, Liz."

Caleb growled, "It's Elizabeth."

Ah, the lady deigned to notice him at last. That pretty rose bloom fled her cheeks in a heartbeat, leaving her white with shock.

Slim spared a glance for Caleb, a quick, polite smile. "Elizabeth, then."

"Um, yes," she managed to murmur. "Next week. I'm looking forward to it."

Slim left. Caleb and Elizabeth stood in uncomfortable silence as actors, staff and lingering patrons scurried around them. Not exactly the reunion he'd hoped for.

He said, "You're looking...You were..." Damn.

"What are you doing here, Caleb?"

No. Not the reunion he'd hoped for at all. Keeping

his expression impassive, he said, "Enjoying a very good play, actually."

She dropped her eyes. "I didn't mean... You surprised me, that's all."

"I know," he said gently. "Listen, I, uh, I guess I shouldn't have horned in with that guy. It's none of my business who you..."

Sure as hell is! the caveman in him hollered.

That bedazzled smile appeared again. She gazed reverentially at the business card she still clutched. "Do you know who that was?"

"Uh..." A dozen malignant responses were perched on the tip of his tongue. He leashed them with an effort. "No. Who?"

"Philip Ogilvy." She stared at him, waiting for recognition. "The Broadway producer!"

He turned to gawk, but the little man had already disappeared. "*That* was Philip Ogilvy?"

She was practically hopping. "*Yes! Yes!* He was impressed says I gave a stirring performance wants me to audition for his new show some revival he's gonna call my agent first thing tomorrow to get the ball rolling *that was Philip Ogilvy!*" She ended on a squeal.

"Don't you think you could muster a little enthusiasm?" Behind Caleb's teasing was the disquieting awareness that he'd never before seen her happy, excited. Her stay with him had had its moments of camaraderie and contentment, especially during the last two weeks, but nothing approaching this manic joy. Was he even capable of making her happy? For her sake he should simply buy her a cup of coffee and walk away. *It's been fun, have a nice life.*

The door to the men's dressing room opened and the actor who'd played Tony emerged. Caleb felt his blood pressure leap till he saw someone step forward to give the actor a big hug and a kiss and a congratulatory box of Godiva chocolates.

"Well, I'll be damned," Caleb muttered, watching the two handsome young men saunter off, practically glued to each other. "That guy's one hell of an actor."

Elizabeth smirked. "Be nice."

"What did I say?" Caleb asked, all innocence.

"Come on." She hooked her arm in his. Even that much contact, muted by layers of goose down and sheepskin, was heaven. "Let's get out of here."

Earlier, the air had felt ponderous and damp with the promise of snow. Now, as they emerged from the warm theater into a frigid February night, glittering snowflakes swirled around them and dusted everything in sight, from parked cars to garbage cans.

Drawing her parka around her throat, she asked, "Do you have the Land Rover here?"

"Yep."

"Good. We won't have to take the subway."

"Where?"

"To my place in Brooklyn."

"Let's go." He led her to a parking garage, where he ransomed his vehicle. Soon they were headed south on Broadway.

She directed, "Go all the way down to the Brooklyn Bridge."

He plunged right in. "I expected to hear from you by now."

She stared straight ahead out the windshield, her breath smoking. "I wasn't ready."

"I guess not. Were you ever going to contact me?"

She sighed heavily. "I needed to work through...a lot."

"I know. I hope you found some answers."

"I did. I think it might be easier talking about it now than it was back then."

"I'm listening." His gloved hands tightened on the steering wheel. Did he really want to hear this?

She began haltingly. "When you...kidnapped me and held me at your estate, it was like I...disappeared in your shadow. It was like everything I'd been up to then—my career, my home, my *life*—they no longer existed...*I* no longer existed."

"It was a strange time for both of us," he said quietly.

"It was different for you. You were the one in control. I was..." She hesitated.

He anticipated her words. *Helpless? Vulnerable? Victimized?*

"I was this...thing being manipulated by you. I had lost all free will, all authority over my own life. All sense of my own identity."

He frowned as her words sank in. He'd heard the same sort of thing from a couple of his buddies who'd been POWs. He fumbled with the wipers and the heater switch, unable to meet her eyes.

She said, "I don't think you understand the effect

you have on people, Caleb. Maybe it's because of your background, all those years in Special Forces, I don't know. You have this overwhelming presence. Of command. Authority. Strength. Standing up to you is like going against a steamroller."

"You managed to bring that steamroller to a screeching halt a few times, as I recall." He smiled, remembering.

"Don't get me wrong, it's not all black-and-white. Those weeks with you taught me to believe in myself on a very basic level—to trust my instincts and my ability to cope with—" she chuckled "—the unexpected, shall we say? Still, I felt this burning need to reestablish myself, assert my independence. That's why I'm working so hard now to jump-start my career."

Her ferocious pride was something he both admired and cursed. "Sweetheart, after watching Mr. Big Shot Producer fawn all over you, I'd say you're on your way. And even if that show doesn't pan out, the next one will. You're damn good at what you do."

She beamed at his praise. "I am, aren't I?" The smile faded as she whipped her head around, finally taking note of the snow-dusted trees and boulders flying past. They were crossing town through Central Park. Headed toward the East Side—not Brooklyn.

"What are you doing?" she demanded.

"Kidnapping you, of course."

She stared at him. "Is that supposed to be funny?"

Real smooth, Trent. "I'm an idiot," he said with a sigh.

She offered no argument.

He said, "I have something I want to show you."

"Caleb—"

"Then I'll take you home. I promise."

Her expression was bleak as she turned from him. Was he doing it again—steamrolling her? And if she was oversensitive, who was to blame?

"Listen, Elizabeth, I'll take you home right now if you want. Right this instant. Just say the word. But I'm asking you, please. There's something—someplace— I'd like you to see." When she hesitated, he added, "It's important to me."

She didn't look at him. "All right."

"Thanks." He reached over and squeezed her gloved hand.

Within a few minutes he was turning onto a block in the east Sixties and scanning ahead for parking. "All right!" he called, spying a minivan's backup lights. "Watch the master parallel park."

He'd always loved this side of New York, the stately row houses with their iron railings, ornate entrances and elegant brownstone facades. He recalled the posh, sprawling apartment on Central Park South where his family had lived until his father's death. As grand as that apartment was, it had never felt like a real home. Even then, at age ten, Caleb had a fondness for these old town houses that exuded warmth and refinement along with a generous dollop of New York history.

As he shuffled the Land Rover into the spot vacated by the van, Elizabeth peered out the window, perusing the neighborhood but saying nothing. He didn't know whether her silence was good or bad. They climbed out and he led her three doors down, through an iron gate and up eight steps to a doorway.

"Whose house is this?" she asked as he fitted the key in the lock. "Is the owner away?"

"I left the heat on, so it should be comfortable." He ushered her into the foyer and flicked a switch. Light from a century-old overhead fixture gleamed on the freshly refinished oak floor, where it wasn't protected with brown paper runners. Through an archway could be seen the large parlor with its green marble fireplace and original wood moldings. Even devoid of furniture, this place was impressive.

He stood in the foyer and watched her amble into the parlor, hands stuffed in her jacket pockets, booted footfalls echoing in the empty space. She lingered before the fireplace and stared down at the one furnishing in the house. His sleeping bag.

She turned and faced him. "What's going on here, Caleb?"

He unbuttoned his jacket. Pulled off his gloves and stuffed them in a pocket. She wasn't going to make this easy for him; he could see that. "I want to show you the rest of the house, Elizabeth. It's four stories, with a terrific backyard and—"

"Did you buy this place?"

He took a deep breath. "Yes. For you."

He saw her eyes widen, but she still didn't smile. In that instant he recalled her hostile reaction in his weight room when he'd offered to buy her new clothes. He'd licked his lips to start over when she spoke up.

"Why did you hunt me down at the theater?"

"I needed to see what was keeping you from me."

"Reconnoitering the enemy?"

"Something like that. And...I figured it was past time I checked out your world, what's important to you." He dragged his fingers through his snow-damp hair. "You're already plenty familiar with my world. It's not like you had any say in the matter."

She seemed to sag a little. He itched to take her in his arms, but something warned him not to rush her. A meow drew their attention to the floor and the young cat crossing the room to inspect the newcomer.

Elizabeth knelt and dropped her shoulder bag. She stripped off her gloves and reached out to stroke the animal, her eyes bright. "Bullwinkle?" She lifted him and examined his distinctive black-and-white markings. She grinned at Caleb. "It's Bullwinkle! He's gotten so big!"

Bullwinkle's tail flicked in annoyance and she released him. But he lingered to nudge her with his nose and rub against her in sinuous feline rapture. This onetime runt had been her favorite of Natasha's litter.

Was it shameless of Caleb to use a dumb beast to soften her up? He smiled crookedly. Was all still fair in love and war? The wry look Elizabeth shot him said she wasn't fooled by Captain Trent's Bullwinkle strategy.

He joined her in the shadowed parlor. "Come outside with me. I want you to see the backyard." He helped her to her feet as Bullwinkle sauntered to the sleeping bag and flopped down for a nap. "We can look at the stars. Remember how we used to look at the stars with my telescope?"

She allowed him to lead her to the back of the house. "Stars? Caleb, it's snowing! Besides, this is big, bright New York City. We wouldn't have much chance of seeing stars on a *clear* night."

He unlocked the back door and she followed him outside. Her breath caught. "It's beautiful."

Snowflakes pirouetted in the wash of light from the windows, lending a magical quality to the scene. The yard was city-small but beautifully landscaped, with a high brick wall for privacy and a three-sided grape arbor that would be bursting with fragrant fruit and huge, shady leaves come summer. He followed as she perused the grounds, their feet crunching on the frozen grass beneath its light blanket of snow.

He said, "I bought this place from one of my clients—he's moving his business out of town and had to sell quickly. I wouldn't say I got it for a song, but since he didn't have to go through a broker, we split the savings. I'm moving my things down next week."

She turned to cast him a curious look. "You're making this your primary residence? I thought you liked running your consulting business from way up in God's country."

He shrugged. "I'll adjust. I like the city well enough. And it's not like you can pursue your acting career a few hundred miles from Broadway. That eight-hour commute is a bitch."

She didn't comment on his presumptuousness. He took that as a good sign and forged ahead. "I figured, since I picked the house, you can choose the furniture. I'll go with anything but flowered chintz. I don't care much for flowered chintz."

"What are you going to do with the house upstate?"

"Keep it. It'll be our country place, like it was originally meant to be. We need *someplace* where we can see the stars. You'll be happy to know I had all the razor wire removed. Now it looks more like a vacation home and less like Leavenworth."

She stopped at the rear of the yard to examine a heavy, ornate wrought-iron bench. Walking behind it, she idly swept powdery snow off the filigreed backrest and turned around to lean against it. She tipped her face up to the sky. In the gloom he could just make out the snowflakes settling on her eyelashes. He wanted to lick them off.

She said, "Speaking of the big house, I can't keep up with our favorite felon's legal shenanigans. What's the latest?"

"Seems Lugh's had a falling out with his lawyers."

"*Again?* Is he going to dump this team, too?"

"Looks that way." Lugh had fired his original lawyers when the judge denied bail. "Poor guy just can't understand why everyone hates him."

She clucked in mock sympathy. "Charming fellow like him."

Caleb said, "When Lugh was holding you...talking about what he'd done to David, what he had in store for you..." He shook his head, fighting the surge of venom even now. "I'd never felt rage like that, Elizabeth. Never. It took everything I had just to keep from throwing myself on the guy and taking him apart. If he hadn't been holding a gun on you..."

She looked away. "I hadn't realized David had confided in him. I hated hearing Lugh ridicule him like that, but at least he corroborated what I'd told you about David and me."

"Elizabeth." He reached out to turn her face to his, make her meet his eyes. "Sweetheart, I didn't need to hear it from that demented son of a bitch. Don't you know I already believed in you?"

He felt her chin tremble under his fingers, and he tenderly stroked her cheek. "I guess I can't say it enough, can I? After everything I put you through."

She placed her hand on his. "You heard Lugh tell how he worked on David, wore him down. Do you still blame yourself for not being more involved? For not running your brother's life for him?"

"No. And that was the hardest part. Giving myself permission to let go of the guilt. David was an adult. Maybe not the strongest-willed guy, maybe not the most mature, but more than capable of making his own decisions."

"But he was still your baby brother," she whispered, kissing his palm and releasing it.

He felt his throat start to close up. She understood. "Yeah. He was still my baby brother."

There was more that needed to be said. He swallowed the knot in his throat, along with a heaping spoonful of pride. "Listen, uh, for what it's worth...my mother was never a healthy woman. She'd been failing for some time. 1 know I implied, way back when, that you were responsible for her death, too. But even then, I never really believed it."

"Caleb." Elizabeth touched his arm. "I never thought you did."

"But it was just so damn petty, so cruel. All of it. I don't blame you for not being able to forgive me."

"Is that what you think? That I haven't been in touch because I can't forgive you?"

"I told you I'd make it up to you, and I meant it."

She nodded toward the rear facade of his new home. "Like this?"

He blinked. "Hell no! Elizabeth—" He stopped, never having heard himself whine before. It was an unsettling sound. He cleared his throat. "Dammit, woman!"

"Well, you must admit, it looks..." She shrugged.

"I don't have to admit a damn thing! I don't give a rat's ass how it looks!"

"Stop swearing at me."

His mouth snapped shut.

"And stop growling."

"I'm not growling. You'll know when I growl."

The witch was smiling! She lifted a slender finger and ran her knuckle up and down his throat. He couldn't have looked away from her bottomless brown eyes if his life depended on it.

Her voice was a low, seductive whisper. He was instantly hard. "It comes from right about here," she said, stroking his throat. "I can feel the vibration. I don't think you're even aware of it."

He clamped his hand around her wrist and felt his Adam's apple leap against her knuckle. "I've waited three long months for you to touch me, Elizabeth. Don't start something you're not willing to finish."

She didn't back down from his fierce gaze. "I don't want you to think the issue is forgiveness, Caleb. I forgave you a long time ago."

His heart banged painfully and he pressed her palm to his chest as if to calm it. He said, "I wish I'd known that."

"I was afraid," she whispered.

He scowled. "Of me?"

"No. Never. I was afraid...of my need for you. Of how desperately I wanted to see you again."

"Elizabeth..." He tried to drag her into his arms, but she held herself away.

She said, "I thought it would be easier once I was on my own, back in my little apartment in Brooklyn, back in the endless grind of auditions and callbacks and rehearsals. I wanted you, but I didn't want to be with you for the wrong reasons."

"What would be the wrong reasons?"

She hugged herself. "When we—when we made love, I was afraid that what I felt for you was...warped. That my emotions were distorted by my dependence on you."

He was catching on. "The Stockholm syndrome. Kind of like what happened to Patty Hearst. Unnatural attachment to your captor."

She nodded.

His first impulse was to dismiss her fears. He knew what he felt for Elizabeth. It was only natural that she return his love. But he also knew it wasn't that simple. Hadn't he just compared her reactions to those of a POW?

Carefully he said, "You've had three months to think about it. What's your take on it now?" Before she could answer, he raised a palm. "I'll wait longer if I have to, Elizabeth. I'll wait as long as it takes for you to feel comfortable about this. About us." He held his breath.

"I don't need any more time." She slid her hands under his open jacket and up his chest. "I love you, Caleb. The longer we're apart, the more miserable I am. I think that means it's the real McCoy."

He groaned and crushed her to him. And kissed her hard until they both nearly collapsed. He whispered into her ear, "I'll do everything in my power to make you happy, sweetheart. Just promise we'll never be apart again. I don't think I could survive it."

He felt her smile. "I can't imagine spending my life with anyone else."

He cradled her face in his palms and licked those snowflakes off her eyelashes. "I'll give you the key to the handcuffs. If I get too overbearing, you have my permission to discipline me in whatever fashion you deem appropriate."

Her grin was lopsided. "Sounds a little kinky to me. I don't know if I'm ready for that, almost-virgin that I am."

"Then that's something else we'll have to work on."
He dropped his hands to stroke her hips through her
long wool skirt. When he gently squeezed her bottom,
she arched toward him with a little gasp. He tilted her
head and took her lips again in a deep, possessive kiss.
His tongue stroked the sweetness of her mouth as his
hands became more aggressive, molding, probing,
searching.

She moaned and tried to get even closer to him,
which was impossible. Breathless, he broke the kiss.
"Elizabeth. Sweetheart." He ran his hands over the
frustratingly pillowy front of her jacket. "Where *are*
they?"

"I never had that complaint before."

He had a choice. He could either strip himself and
Elizabeth naked and let the neighbors find their frozen
cadavers locked together in the morning, or he could
try to drag her inside to his sleeping bag before he exploded.

Or he could let instinct take over.

"Caleb, what...?" she said over her shoulder as he
turned her around to face the back of the iron bench.

He pulled the sides of his shearling jacket around
her, enveloping her in his heat. "I need you, Elizabeth." He held her firmly by the hips and let her feel
the erection that hammered her right through their
clothes. "I need you now." She shuddered and he felt
her tension melt as she wriggled back against him.

He yanked her skirt up to her waist. She sucked in a
sharp breath as he ran his icy hands over her hot, satin
skin. Further exploration revealed she wore silky bi-

kini panties and thigh-high stockings that stayed up all by themselves, without garters. He'd long ago concluded that women's underthings were magic. No use trying to figure them out.

He hooked his thumbs in her panties and pulled them down. After a few moments struggling to get them over her cowboy boots, he jammed them in his pocket.

"Caleb...oh, I missed you so much," she whimpered as he unzipped and freed himself. He pulled her against him, flesh to flesh, and was rewarded by her strangled sob and the restless movements that betrayed her hunger. He reached around her hip and slid his fingers into the soft hair and the silky folds it shielded. She was so hot, so slick and ready!

Desperate little cries escaped her. He prayed he'd be able to rein in his own galloping need long enough to give her pleasure. "Sweetheart, I love you so much," he murmured into her ear. Quickly retrieving a condom from his wallet, he sheathed himself, then tilted her hips and felt her slippery heat welcome him.

He surged into her. Her hoarse scream bounced off the brick walls surrounding them. He forced himself to remain still as her tight flesh rippled around him.

"Elizabeth...am I hurting you?" She was, after all, an almost-virgin.

"No! No!" she gasped. "It's just...so good. Too good."

Didn't he know it. She angled herself to receive him fully, her knuckles white on the bench. The unspoken invitation sparked a primitive response from deep within him. He brushed her hair off her neck and closed his teeth on the tender skin. Just hard enough to hold her, claim her, stamp her as his as he buried himself to the hilt.

He reared up, staggered by the stark physical pleasure that was nearly painful in its intensity...by the boundless depth of his love for this woman. He felt raw and exposed and cleansed by that love.

He continued to caress her intimately, determined to give her the same pleasure she gave him. He urged her to move with him, and she did, eagerly meeting his deep, fierce thrusts, the cold forgotten as they generated their own heat.

Sharp, panting gasps heralded her climax, turning to shrill cries as she bucked against him. He let himself go then, let her rhythmic, clutching release trigger his own. His shout echoed off the walls as he gave himself over to the pure pumping energy that consumed him.

She slumped and he held her up, both of them trembling and slick with sweat. She said hoarsely, "I hear you can also do this in a bed."

"You don't say." He tidied up and straightened their clothing, his heart still pounding like a jackhammer. "Have to give that a try sometime."

She turned in his arms and they clung to each other for a shaky kiss. She said, "We were a little loud. What'll the neighbors think?"

"This is New York. They'll think I was mugging you."

"Rhythmically?"

He wagged his eyebrows and kissed her again. She

snuggled against him as he draped an arm over her shoulder, and together they began to stagger back toward the house.

She said, "You kept your promise. Thanks."

"My promise?"

"To protect me the next time we made love, remember?"

"Oh, that. No problem, sweetheart. I laid in four dozen of the damn things."

Her eyebrows shot up.

He said, "We're well stocked with all the essential ingredients of a proper reunion. Trojans. Rémy Martin. Friskies Buffet."

"You'll have to go out again. I prefer my Friskies Buffet on lightly buttered toast points."

"Guess I should've gone grocery shopping, huh?"

"Phone connected?"

"Of course."

"All is not lost. Pizza or Chinese?"

"Let's order Chinese. I have this fantasy about feeding you lo mein in bed."

"What bed?"

"Oh yeah. Well, the way I figure it, we can work up to this bed thing in stages. Next step—sleeping bag."

"Does it fit two?"

He held the door open for her. "We'll find out."

EVER HAD ONE OF THOSE DAYS?

TO DO:

☑ late for a super-important meeting, you discover the cat has eaten your panty hose

☑ while you work through lunch, the rest of the gang goes out and finds a one-hour, once-in-a-lifetime 90% off sale at the most exclusive store in town (Oh, and they also get to meet Brad Pitt who's filming a movie across the street.)

☑ you discover that your intimate phone call with your boyfriend was on company-wide intercom

☑ finally at the end of a long and exasperating day, you escape from it all with an entertaining, humorous and always romantic Love & Laughter book!

ENJOY
LOVE & LAUGHTER™
EVERY DAY!

For a preview, turn the page....

Here's a sneak peek at
Colleen Collins's RIGHT CHEST, WRONG NAME
Available August 1997...

———————

"DARLING, YOU SOUND like a broken cappuccino machine," murmured Charlotte, her voice oozing disapproval.

Russell juggled the receiver while attempting to sit up in bed, but couldn't. If he *sounded* like a wreck over the phone, he could only imagine what he looked like.

"What mischief did you and your friends get into at your bachelor's party last night?" she continued.

She always had a way of saying "your friends" as though they were a pack of degenerate water buffalo. Professors deserved to be several notches higher up on the food chain, he thought. Which he would have said if his tongue wasn't swollen to twice its size.

"You didn't do anything...bad...did you, Russell?"

"Bad." His laugh came out like a bark.

"Bad as in *naughty*."

He heard her piqued tone but knew she'd never admit to such a base emotion as jealousy. Charlotte Maday, the woman he was to wed in a week, came from a family who bled blue. Exhibiting raw emotion was akin to burping in public.

After agreeing to be at her parents' pool party by noon, he untangled himself from the bed sheets and stumbled to the bathroom.

"Pool party," he reminded himself. He'd put on his best front and accommodate Char's request. Make the family rounds, exchange a few pleasantries, play the role she liked best: the erudite, cultured English literature professor. After fulfilling his duties, he'd slink into some lawn chair, preferably one in the shade, and nurse his hangover.

He tossed back a few aspirin and splashed cold water on his face. Grappling for a towel, he squinted into the mirror.

Then he jerked upright and stared at his reflection, blinking back drops of water. "Good Lord. They stuck me in a wind tunnel."

His hair, usually neatly parted and combed, sprang from his head as though he'd been struck by lightning. "Can too many Wild Turkeys do that?" he asked himself as he stared with horror at his reflection.

Something caught his eye in the mirror. Russell's gaze dropped.

"What in the—"

Over his pectoral muscle was a small patch of white. A bandage. Gingerly, he pulled it off.

Underneath, on his skin, was not a wound but a small, neat drawing.

"A red heart?" His voice cracked on the word *heart*. Something—a word?—was scrawled across it.

"Good Lord," he croaked. "I got a tattoo. A heart tattoo with the name Liz on it."

Not Charlotte. Liz!

And the Winner Is...
You!

...when you pick up these great titles
from our new promotion at your
favorite retail outlet this June!

Diana Palmer
The Case of the Mesmerizing Boss

Betty Neels
The Convenient Wife

Annette Broadrick
Irresistible

Emma Darcy
A Wedding to Remember

Rachel Lee
Lost Warriors

Marie Ferrarella
Father Goose

HARLEQUIN®   **Silhouette®**

Take 4 bestselling love stories FREE

Plus get a FREE surprise gift!

Special Limited-time Offer

Mail to Harlequin Reader Service®

> P.O. Box 609
> Fort Erie, Ontario
> L2A 5X3

YES! Please send me 4 free Harlequin Temptation® novels and my free surprise gift. Then send me 4 brand-new novels every month, which I will receive before they appear in bookstores. Bill me at the low price of $3.34 each plus 25¢ delivery and GST.* That's the complete price and a savings of over 10% off the cover prices—quite a bargain! I understand that accepting the books and gift places me under no obligation ever to buy any books. I can always return a shipment and cancel at any time. Even if I never buy another book from Harlequin, the 4 free books and the surprise gift are mine to keep forever.

342 BPA A3UG

Name	(PLEASE PRINT)
Address	Apt. No.
City	Province	Postal Code

This offer is limited to one order per household and not valid to present Harlequin Temptation® subscribers. *Terms and prices are subject to change without notice. Canadian residents will be charged applicable provincial taxes and GST.

CTEMP-696

FORTUNE COOKIE

Breathtaking romance is predicted in your future with Harlequin's newest collection: Fortune Cookie.

Three of your favorite Harlequin authors, Janice Kaiser, Margaret St. George and M.J. Rodgers will regale you with the romantic adventures of three heroines who are promised fame, fortune, danger and intrigue when they crack open their fortune cookies on a fateful night at a Chinese restaurant.

Join in the adventure with your own personalized fortune, inserted in every book!

Don't miss this exciting new collection!

Available in September wherever Harlequin books are sold.

HARLEQUIN®

Let's Celebrate!

LOVE & LAUGHTER™

invites you to
the party of the season!

Grab your popcorn and be prepared to laugh as we celebrate with **LOVE & LAUGHTER**.

Harlequin's newest series is going Hollywood!

Let us make you laugh with three months of terrific books, authors and romance, plus a chance to win a FREE 15-copy video collection of the best romantic comedies ever made.

For more details look in the back pages of any Love & Laughter title, from July to September, at your favorite retail outlet.

Don't forget the popcorn!

Available wherever
Harlequin books are sold.

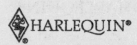

HARLEQUIN®

Look us up on-line at: http://www.romance.net

LLCELEB

HE SAID

SHE SAID

Explore the mystery of male/female communication in this extraordinary new book from two of your favorite Harlequin authors.

Jasmine Cresswell and Margaret St. George bring you the exciting story of two romantic adversaries—each from their own point of view!

DEV'S STORY. CATHY'S STORY.
As he sees it. As she sees it.
Both sides of the story!

The heat is definitely on, and these two can't stay out of the kitchen!

Don't miss **HE SAID, SHE SAID.**
Available in July wherever Harlequin books are sold.

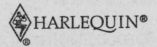

HARLEQUIN®

HARLEQUIN WOMEN KNOW ROMANCE WHEN THEY SEE IT.

And they'll see it on **ROMANCE CLASSICS**, the new 24-hour TV channel devoted to romantic movies and original programs like the special **Harlequin** Showcase of Authors & Stories.

The **Harlequin** Showcase of Authors & Stories introduces you to many of your favorite romance authors in a program developed exclusively for Harlequin readers.

Watch for the **Harlequin** Showcase of **Authors & Stories** series beginning in the summer of 1997.

ROMANCE CLASSICS

If you're not receiving ROMANCE CLASSICS, call your local cable operator or satellite provider and ask for it today!

Escape to the network of your dreams.

As Seen on TV!

Free Gift Offer

With a Free Gift proof-of-purchase
from any Harlequin® book, you can receive
a beautiful cubic zirconia pendant.

This stunning marquise-shaped stone is a genuine cubic
zirconia—accented by an 18" gold tone necklace.
(Approximate retail value $19.95)

Send for yours today...
compliments of ✦ HARLEQUIN®

To receive your free gift, a cubic zirconia pendant, send us one original proof-of-purchase, photocopies not accepted, from the back of any Harlequin Romance®, Harlequin Presents®, Harlequin Temptation®, Harlequin Superromance®, Harlequin Intrigue®, Harlequin American Romance®, or Harlequin Historicals® title available at your favorite retail outlet, together with the Free Gift Certificate, plus a check or money order for $1.65 U.S./$2.15 CAN. (do not send cash) to cover postage and handling, payable to Harlequin Free Gift Offer. We will send you the specified gift. Allow 6 to 8 weeks for delivery. Offer good until December 31, 1997, or while quantities last. Offer valid in the U.S. and Canada only.

Free Gift Certificate

Name: _____

Address: _____

City: _____ State/Province: _____ Zip/Postal Code: _____

Mail this certificate, one proof-of-purchase and a check or money order for postage and handling to: HARLEQUIN FREE GIFT OFFER 1997. In the U.S.: 3010 Walden Avenue, P.O. Box 9071, Buffalo NY 14269-9057. In Canada: P.O. Box 604, Fort Erie, Ontario L2Z 5X3.

FREE GIFT OFFER   084-KEZ

ONE PROOF-OF-PURCHASE
To collect your fabulous FREE GIFT, a cubic zirconia pendant, you must include this
original proof-of-purchase for each gift with the properly completed Free Gift Certificate.

084-KEZR